The Angel of Shadwell

A Case for Inspector Noridel

Jonathan Templar

First Edition

ISBN: 1-938644-04-2
ISBN-13: 978-1-938644-04-7

Nightscape Press, LLP
http://www.nightscapepress.com

To Frances and Maebh

For everything.

PROLOGUE

It awoke into darkness and knew immediately that something was missing.

It searched its unfamiliar surroundings but could not find what it had lost.

So it started to hunt for a new one.

1.
THE HOUSE OF POPPY

Limehouse, Low London
October 4th, 83 A.V (Anno Victoria)

Thaddeus Noridel, son of the once eminent physician, Zeus Noridel, brother to Ishmael and Daniel (deceased) and Detective Inspector in the Eternal Queen's Domestic Constabulary inhaled from the opium pipe until his face was puce and his cheeks were fit to burst.

He let the smoke drift into the pleasure centres of his brain, allowed narcotic tendrils to wrap themselves around his sanity and squeeze. Then he let the smoke out, a long exhalation like a dampened dragon.

For a while he sat, quite senseless. Then his mind returned to his body, partially at any rate, and he called Lee over.

Lee was taller than he should have been, the lower parts of his legs removed, by accident or design Noridel had never asked, and replaced by spring-loaded pistons that allowed him to bounce around his surroundings and tower over his visitors. His face had been augmented as well, a telescopic left eye replacing the one he had been born with, loose segments rattling as he bounced, extending and retracting without notice. Lee always wore flowing silk robes which concealed the rest of his body, Noridel could never know how much of what lay underneath was still Lee and how much was the work of his Flesh Tailor.

Lee bent his strange head toward Noridel.

"*Lee,*" Noridel squeaked, the high pitch of his voice surprising him. He swallowed it back down and tried again. "Lee," he said, and it sounded better, "this is a particularly potent potion you've brewed. A new supplier?"

Lee bowed dutifully. "Always we seek only the very finest of poppy tears. I am glad that the Inspector finds favour."

"Balls to the *Inspector* business, Lee. As I've said a hundred or more times, as soon as I pass through the doorway of your sordid little hovel I leave all trace of my professional identity behind. I am a simple slave to the pipe, nothing more, and you must address me as such."

"Of course, Inspector."

"Now you're just toying with me, Lee."

"I serve at the Inspector's pleasure. My family

have long held the opinion that to best serve the will of the angels one must occasionally clip their wings."

Noridel took in another mouthful of the potent opium.

"You can keep your eastern philosophy to yourself as well. You and your bloody Confucius. He didn't do you much good when the Empire came a calling did he?" Noridel's voice had started to slur.

"No, he did not, Inspector." Lee's telescopic eye extended itself accidentally so that it was almost in Noridel's face. He pushed it back in with some effort. "The Empire of the Eternal Queen swept across our land like the sharpest of scythes. But all must remember: even the sharpest of blades can quickly be blunted."

"And there you go again with the mystical mumbo. I've seen you, Lee, down in the gambler's pits placing half your living wage on some random bookie's choice in the mecha-hound fights. I hear tell that you adopt a very different philosophy when you've got your cash at stake."

Lee laughed, warmly. "Then we both choose to present a professional face to the world that hides the one we show when we are at play."

"Amen to that, my friend," Noridel said.

A fat and lazily stoned man was sitting opposite Noridel, listening to all of this. "I say," he called as Lee trotted off to care for the well being of other customers. "Are you really one of the constabulary?"

"Shhh!" Noridel put a finger to his mouth, missed, and then giggled like a school girl.

"I can't say I find myself comfortable undertaking

illicit activities in the knowledge that I'm sitting opposite a copper."

"It's perfectly all right, my fat friend. I can assure you that any interest I hold in this den of iniquity is purely for my own pleasure. The only person at risk due to my presence here is my good self."

The fat man wobbled. "Why on earth would you risk your very life to be here? Surely the penalty for narcotic abuse amongst the constabulary is severe in the extreme?"

"Severe indeed. Ha! Were I to be discovered here, my very life would indeed be forfeit. Such are the risks we take, we desperate addicts of the poppy." A shadow came across Noridel's face, a sudden darkening of his mood. "It's all my father's fault, him and his bloody laudanum. Had I not been raised in a household where the very drug that would be my downfall was applied to each and every one of us as a cure-all tonic, then I would still be on the straight and narrow today. Had I not been raised by a woman who had become herself an unwilling slave to the needle, a slave whose chains had been forged by her own husband in the name of medical well being. To hell with him, and them! And to hell with the constabulary and the cursed Queen; long may her porcine extremities remain frozen."

"Now steady on," fatty said, raising his bulk from the complicated arrangement of cushions that supported him. "One must keep thoughts and feelings of this nature quiet; one never knows whom we are espousing them."

"Why should I care?" Noridel said petulantly.

"The Empire has eyes and ears and it has them

everywhere. To talk in such a way could be considered sedition."

"Good. Then sedition it is! Why should I remain quiet about the blight and the corruption I see on a daily basis? An empire? More like a ruddy bee hive, all of us dancing attendance to our bloated monstrosity of a Queen bee."

The fat man pondered for a few moments, then shuffled his unpleasant bulk across to Noridel.

"You are not alone in the way you think," he said through clenched teeth.

"I should bloody well hope not, unless the rest of the country is populated solely by idiots, which I wouldn't be at all surprised to discover was indeed the case."

"There are lots of people, people in all sort of positions of power, who have, shall we say, concerns at the way the Empire is being run. And with those who are running it."

"And this should concern me *why*?"

"Have you any idea who I am?"

"If your appearance is anything to go by, I believe that you are a man with a variety of vices and little or no control over any of them." Noridel poked the man hard in his generous belly. "Either that or you are with child and, unless I am mistaken, even the most skilled of Professor Varteck's flesh farmers have yet to master that particular miracle."

The fat man ignored the insults. "I am the Member of Parliament for Battersea South," he half whispered, half proudly pronounced.

"A member of the House, reclining *here*, in a back street opium pit? Whoever would have imagined it," Noridel said with a voice dripping sarcasm.

"Enough of your bile, Inspector. I and others like me are attempting to construct a new and radically alternative approach to the problems the Empire is facing both domestically and in the newly conquered lands. We are moving slowly, gaining new supporters as we go. People in positions of power and influence who will be vital to our cause if and when we choose to act. As a high ranking officer of the constabulary, you could be a very useful addition to that cause."

"I've never been much of one for causes…"

"Your most passionate and eloquent words of condemnation suggested otherwise. Will you consider meeting with some of us, quietly and discreetly, so that we can detail the extent of our objections, allow you to consider the alternatives we are creating? Perhaps we may persuade you to join us in our intentions."

"Let me see if I have this clear," Noridel said. "You, the Right Honourable Member of Her Majesty's Parliament for Battersea South are asking me, a Detective Inspector in Her Majesty's Domestic Constabulary, to attend a meeting with other parties not presently named, the purpose of said meeting to discuss active sedition and to draw up plans to overthrow the Eternal Queen's rule by act of revolution?"

The fat politician nodded his flabby head. "In a manner of speaking, I suppose I am, yes."

Noridel turned to the giant ceramic bong from which the opium pipe was protruding. "Did you get all of that, Cecil?"

The bong spun around, accompanied by a

whirring, clicking, mechanical sound. "Roger, Roger, Inspector. All duly recorded and ready to be played back at a moment's notice. 'Ow bloody good am I then, eh?"

The top of the bong opened to reveal a revolving wax cylinder into which a number of groves had been scratched by a stylus arm.

"This is Cecil," Noridel indicated the bong. "He's my portable phonograph. He has just made a recording of everything you have said, Mr John Aubrey Waites. Yes, I know exactly who you are, sir."

Waites trembled, wobbled, his fleshy skin turning pale. "You... this is entrapment, surely? I was just having a simple conversation, humouring what I believed to be a nonsensical drug addict in the throes of an opiate delirium. I certainly didn't *mean* any of what I said, surely you must see that!"

"On the contrary, *sir*, you have been watched very carefully for several months by agents of Her Majesty's Most Secret Service and your seditious ways have been duly noted. All that was required was evidence that would convict you in a court of law, evidence which I, as a serving officer in the constabulary, was only too happy to assist in obtaining."

The quiet of the smoky opium den was broken by the heavy footfalls of bobbies as they descended the wooden steps, cuffs in hand, their tall domed helmets almost touching the low fragile ceiling. Noridel could see Lee backing away to the darkest corner of the hall, wincing as he watched the clumsy movements of the coppers.

"You can't do this," Waites protested as steel

handcuffs that could contain a mountain gorilla were roughly clamped around his oversized wrists, squeezing the corpulent flesh. "I am a very important man, I am an elected official! You can't just drag me away like some kind of common or garden miscreant!"

Noridel stood and faced the man, letting the grubby shroud that he had wrapped around himself fall to the floor revealing his pristine clothing beneath.

"On the contrary, sir, a common miscreant is *exactly* what you are. By virtue of your arrest you are stripped of all rights and privileges bestowed upon members of the House. You are now considered to be a common citizen and as such all assets and premises owned by yourself and your direct family line are now the property of Her Majesty until such time as you are proved to be innocent of any charges that have been or will be made against you. You will be taken from here and placed into the custody of the Most Secret Service, under whose authority any and all steps considered appropriate can and will be taken to ensure your full cooperation in their ongoing investigation."

"Please," Waites said, falling to his knees. "I don't deserve this. I'm a good man; I only want the best for my constituents."

"That is not for me to judge. But suffice it to say, sir, I seldom have the time or the inclination to listen to the empty entreaties of those who would dampen their intelligence with the poison of the poppy pipes. Take him away, constables."

The wailing prisoner was escorted with some difficulty up the narrow staircase and into custody.

"He was a bit of a one, weren't 'e sir?" the ceramic bong said in a cockney metal voice.

"He certainly was, Cecil. Let us hope that his fate will serve as a lesson to others that dare plan treason against Her Majesty's rule."

"Too right, sir. I ain't got no time for traitors. Fat bastards, either."

There was a lighter footfall on the wooden steps and Sergeant Crayford poked her head into the den.

"Blimey, sir, it stinks something rotten down here."

"Good evening, Sergeant. I'm glad that your assistance was not required."

Crayford walked over, fanning the smoke away from her face and twitching her button nose with disgust. "Yes sir, me an' all. Why anyone would want to waste their lives away wallowing in this filth, I will never know."

"The pleasure of the pipe once tasted can never be forgotten. These opium addicts rarely choose to become slaves to its charms, Crayford. Like so many vices, it is easier to board the train of pleasure than it is to disembark."

"So you say," she sniffed. "So how come *you* can smoke this stuff and not become addicted then?"

"The story I told Waites was at least partially true. Always cloud your lies in truth, Crayford, if you want them to be believed. My father did indeed prescribe the regular injection of laudanum for the members of his family. My brothers and I must have had more of the filthy mixture running through our veins than we did our life blood by the time we turned twelve. A mouthful of opium hardly compares."

"He was a bit of a nutcase, your dad, I take it."

"It would be safe for you to make that assumption, Crayford. "

As they left the opium den, they passed by Lee, who was cowering in the doorway, his telescopic eye bulging. "Thank you for your assistance, Lee. If at any time I can return the favour, be certain to call upon me."

"The greatest favour you can grant me, Inspector, is to stay as far away from my business as possible for any man to be."

"That I would do, Lee, were your business of a legitimate nature. Sadly, I am the price you must pay for peddling your abhorrent wares."

"Often I believe this to be a price too high to pay," Lee bounced softly up and down on his springs, his augmented eye wobbling.

"Then I will be the first to wish you success in your next profession," Noridel returned the bow and left Lee to clean up his mess.

"He must hate the very sight of you, sir," Crayford smirked as the only slightly fresher air of the London streets replaced the opium fumes.

"Who, Lee? I consider him to be one of my closest friends, Crayford. And the man really does seem to get hold of the most incredible poppy, the finest in all of Low London."

They crossed the narrow cobbles and handed the now snoozing Cecil to one of the Most Secret Service agents to be placed in a black ornithopter that would take Waites and the evidence of his misdeeds to some secret and terrible location away from prying eyes and ears. Noridel always ensured he was particularly helpful and attentive to the

MSS. He hoped to one day join their number, but was aware that there were certain *incidents* in his past that would probably prevent that from ever happening.

A pity.

"A job well done, Crayford. Time to hit the hay, I think."

"I'm afraid not, sir. We had a wire while you were down in the opium pit. There's been a murder over at the docks, your presence is requested."

Noridel whispered something uncharacteristically crude under his breath.

2.
MURDER AT THE DOCKS

The body had been found at Shadwell docks, the very worst place for a crime to be discovered.

In times past, the low docks had dealt only with ships that traversed the long and treacherous channels of the River Thames. Now, vast man-made structures towered upwards into the sky, eclipsing the sun in that corner of London. Mooring platforms had been erected for the freight zeppelins to deliver their loads, the vast helium-filled ships circling the air awaiting their turn to dock. The many levels beneath were a warren of cargo holds and storage bays, elevators and cages constantly in motion taking goods plundered from foreign lands to the dispatch areas far below. The sound of cogs screeching and gears whining could, and often did, deafen the unprepared visitor.

The air was thick with helium vapours, gas that constantly leaked from the massive refuelling tanks. Hot steam shot from pipes to scald the unwary, and thick condensation coated each surface, turning every ladder and scaffold into a potential death trap.

If the environment itself was not enough of a trial for an investigating officer, Shadwell was organised like an empire all of its own, the Dockers following their own set of laws and conventions that made it nigh on impossible for outsiders to impose their own. The two Guilds, those of the Flesh and the Clockwork, had their own rules, their own hierarchies and their own unfathomable customs.

When Her Majesty's Constabulary walked here, they did so upon eggshells.

The body had been found on one of the mid-levels, exposed to all who happened to pass. There had been no attempt to conceal it, nor disguise the horrific wounds that had been inflicted on the victim. He had simply been left to the rusting elements.

It had been a gaggle of decrepit whores who found him, whores amongst the very few who were desperate enough to creep through the warren of the working docks in search of trade rather than seek it in the public houses and back alleys that surrounded them. There they would find competition from both flesh and automata, and one look at the unfortunates was enough to appreciate their desire to avoid any competition for their services.

Inspector Noridel hated whores.

He knew that many of the wretched women had little choice but to surrender their dignity to survive in a cruel and unsympathetic world, but the construction fields were littered with workhouses that offered them shelter and food. There were men without husbands and children without mothers or nursemaids. To choose instead to offer oneself to a stranger for a handful of coins, to Noridel this was the choice of the slovenly coward, the slattern. He found it hard to swallow his bile whenever he had cause to interrogate such creatures.

Sadly, his job meant this was rather a regular occurrence.

This trio were particularly low examples of the oldest profession. One tall, one fat, one thin, as if they were characters from some perverted nursery rhythm, all three draped in tattered finery that might well have been pilfered from a corpse, and not a fresh one at that.

The tall one was missing most of her nose, the jagged trace of stitches around her face suggested violence rather than syphilis, but she had teeth, a few at least, which was more than her companions could boast. The fat one had a face distorted by numerous growths that were surely the sign of something dark and inoperable. The thin one rocked backwards and forwards constantly, and dribbled from a corner of her mouth as she did so, her eyes devoid of anything approaching intelligence. Noridel wondered when she had last eaten, but found he didn't really care what the answer was.

"There was no one else in the area when you found the deceased?" Noridel asked them, barely concealing his distaste.

The tall and the fat looked at each other. A silent conspiracy played across their faces.

"Come on, tell me what you saw or we'll take a quick trip down to Bedlam, the three of us, and see what accommodation they can provide for your shambolic friend here."

Noridel's an upper middle-class nightmare profession had provided him with sufficient knowledge of the depths of depravity the lower elements of society could sink to, so it wasn't a huge leap for him to imagine the benefits for two fading prostitutes of having an idiot colleague without the capacity to resist or complain.

"Now that ain't fair," the fat one spat, her breath fetid.

"We came told you what we'd found, we didn't have to do that, did we?" the thin one added.

"I am sure that your altruism is in no way motivated by the attention your sordid little ménage a trios will attract subsequent to news of your discovery hitting the streets."

The tall one spat something black and poisonous to the floor at his feet.

"What did you see?" Noridel asked again.

"It were an angel," Tall said, widening her eyes to ensure the impact of her words was echoed by her face.

"*An angel?*" Noridel repeated. He hadn't been expecting that.

They both nodded enthusiastically.

"He were eight feet tall if he were an inch," said

Fat.

"And he shone, he did. Shone like the sun," added Tall.

"And you saw him clearly, this *angel?*"

"We all did. He were standing over the body, blood all over his hands. And he were holding something up to his chest, like this," Tall demonstrated, holding her hands together over her left breast. "Then he were off, fast as lightening. Well, we were so scared we was ready to piss our petticoats. But he weren't interested in the likes of us."

And who could blame him.

"So, why do you say he was an angel?"

"Well he was gold weren't he?"

"Gold?"

"Like I said. Gold. Shining like a new shilling, he was."

"His clothes were gold, you mean?"

"No, his face! He were made of gold."

"Made of gold?"

She shrugged. "Might've been bronze I suppose."

Fat nodded at this. "Yeah, bronze, like them statutes up there in Trafalgar. And there were the dents an' all."

"Dents?" Noridel asked, now completely perplexed.

"Yeah, he had dents on his 'ed, big ones. I figure it were because of how he'd like...fallen,"

"What, fallen over?" Tall said.

Fat slapped her arm. "No, you halfwit! *Fallen*. From 'eaven, like."

Noridel let them go. As unreliable a trio of witnesses as he had ever had the misfortune to encounter. Let them have their evening of fame in the dank drinking holes that polluted the area. That fame would last no longer than their morning hangover.

Any clues to be found on the unfortunate victim were only likely to be discovered back at the station.

With a heavy heart, Noridel made his way back, fully aware that Doctor Pink would be eagerly awaiting him.

3.
DR PINK

The East End of Low London was hardly the best spot in the Empire to be a copper, but at the same time it was far from the worst. It was too close to the construction sites that lined the Thames down into the Kentish wastelands, so a thick sulphurous cloud hung over the region from dusk to the sometimes barely discernible dawn and there was a smell that you could never scrape from your nostrils.

The smell of progress, or so the public were constantly told.

Crime was rife, but mainly consisted of minor

offences, and much of this didn't reach the eyes or ears of the law. The Guilds reigned supreme at the docks, kept their own form of order and justice and the constabulary were largely happy to let them go about it.

Shadwell Station served as more of a barracks than a headquarters. The vast majority of the constabulary housed within its walls were simple constables of the watch, the bobbies, whose job it was to be out and about on the streets, high visibility at all times, there to prevent not to detect.

Noridel was one of only two inspectors based in the building, which stretched over three floors, including the cellar, and always stunk of tobacco and socks. The other Inspector was named Blithe and seemed only to exist as a name inscribed on his office door and the occasional sighting of a tall pale man who answered to the same name and was occasionally spotted eating kippers in the canteen. Noridel knew him by sight but had spoken to him only half a dozen times during the two years they had worked in the same building, usually to ask who the bloody hell he was. Such were the vagaries of the constabulary.

What the Shadwell Station did hold, and what Noridel wished beyond measure that it didn't, was the district morgue.

Tonight's victim had found his terminal home on a stone slab in said morgue. The coroner, Doctor Pink, hovered over it wielding a gore stained instrument. His apron was smeared with the dead man's blood.

The good doctor never looked happier than when he was up to his elbows in entrails.

There were all sorts of rumours about Pink, that he was an ex-convict who had learnt the art of autopsy whilst being detained at Her Eternal Majesty's pleasure, or that he had been a member if the ill-fated initial incursion into the Khyber Pass that had led to the legendary massacre, the details of which could curl the toes of even the most hardened sadist. The story was that Pink had gone mad treating the wounds of the thousands of mutilated men under his care and now would only ever raise a knife to flesh that had already turned blue on the slab.

Noridel rather thought that Pink himself had started these rumours. He certainly had a flair for the dramatic. And a taste for the gin.

"This is certainly one for the memoirs," Pink said with a smile only partially obscured by his magnificent moustache.

"Unusual?" Noridel said, his own mouth obscured by his handkerchief, dipped in smelling salts to help him avoid the stench of death that hung in the cellars that formed Doctor Pink's domain. Coming to the cellars really did feel like a descent into hell. The low ceilings were lit only by the dullest of lamp light, light that did little but get swallowed by dark green tiles that lined the upper walls. The gloom did at least obscure the rows of the dead covered in soiled sheets and the jars that lined the shelves, jars that contained fermenting fragments of many a past tenant. The old stone floor was damp, and you felt the cold in your chest within moments of entering the chamber.

"I should say so," Pink said. "This poor fellow has had his sodding heart removed. Now, that alone isn't something to get excited about, we had a whole spate of such murders just last year, brigands selling fresh organs to the hybrid farms. All hushed up of course, but I saw a lot of wounds inflicted with the aim of removing organs, and they were nothing like this atrocity."

"What makes this special?"

"You see the damage to the rib cage here?" Doctor Pink pointed with the jagged blade of his instrument. Noridel wished he wouldn't. He wasn't a queasy man, as such, but he preferred to see the garish details of a murder detailed in the form of Pink's detailed anatomical diagrams rather than freshly dissected flesh.

The same information but none of the stench.

"It would be hard to miss," Noridel said. And indeed it would. The trunk of the unfortunate victim had been parted, the rib cage pulled open as if it were the door to a bird cage. There was terrible damage to the innards beneath. Noridel gagged.

"This man has been torn apart, Noridel. Not sliced, not hacked. Torn. The heart was ripped out of him; there was nothing surgical about its removal, no hint of precision. It'll be useless now, unless the aggressor was planning to eat it with a nice plate of onions."

"What could exert such force?"

"Off the top of me head, I've no idea. What I can tell you is that some form of tool or mechanism was used."

"How can you be certain?"

Pink slid a metal tray in front of him. There were flakes of something inorganic amongst the pools of gore. "See that? Rust. Found it all over the victim's

chest."
Rust.
From a Golden Angel?

~

Noridel was glad to see his office, doubly glad to see Sergeant Crayford. He had sent her directly to the station rather than the crime scene as he liked her perspective to be slightly askew from his own. If they saw the same thing, they might think the same thoughts. If one of them had to piece together the details only from a report, they might ask questions that would otherwise have gone unasked.

Crayford was the only female in the constabulary.

She had disguised herself as a man to enrol at the academy; defying both the law and the natural order of the sexes as Her Majesty the Eternal Queen had defined them. Within hours, her deception had been uncovered and she had been the victim of a most indelicate and prolonged "punishment" at the hands of her fellow trainees.

The following morning, still bruised and battered but utterly defiant, she had returned to the academy disguised in an identical manner. But on this occasion the Academy Director, who had lost three limbs and an eye while in combat reclaiming the North American colonies and was therefore well placed to recognise both courage and determination, had prevented any additional reprisals and declared that every other trainee for the constabulary must treat her as though she were a male and an equal or face expulsion themselves.

Crayford had overcome a year of relentless hostility to graduate. After only a year as a constable, she had been promoted to Sergeant. She was brilliant, intuitive, and completely illegal in the eyes of the law. Nobody mentioned publically that she was a member of the fairer sex. The establishment had simply turned a blind eye.

"Morning, sir," she said, not looking up from the jungle of paper that constituted her desk.

"Is it, Crayford? I've lost any sense of the bloody time. Any identification on our victim?"

"I reckon so. We have one Ezekiel Mott, aged twenty-eight, employed at Shadwell as a manual winder for the Unloading Fourth. He's no one. No family, no prior offences."

"How did we get his name?"

"Couple of his colleagues saw him being taken out. What was left of the blighter, anyway."

"Anything useful from them?"

"Not a sausage, I'm afraid, sir. He was slow, they said." She tapped her head. "Slow up here. He'd been at the docks for years, night shift. Wouldn't say boo to a goose, normally. That's all I've got."

Noridel sat down in his chair, the distressed leather moulded around his trim shape through years of use.

"Why take his heart, Crayford?"

"To sell it to the hybrid farms?"

"Not according to Dr Pink."

"Some sort of ritual, then?"

"Symbolic of what though, Crayford? Did our Mr Mott have a spurned lover somewhere? It seems a rather severe punishment."

"Could it be Guild related?"

"It's possible I suppose, but there's been no suggestion of any recent antagonism between them, and it's far too overt an act for it to be a punishment killing. He'd just have been thrown into the Dead Thames if that had been the case. But look into it, speak to the Guilds, ruffle a few feathers in that inimitable fashion of yours."

"Yes, sir." Crayford rose from her desk, putting on her long coat and her pork pie hat. She was always obviously a woman, but it tended to work best if she didn't advertise her gender too overtly. "You look as if there's something bothering you, sir?"

Noridel looked up. He had indeed been drifting. "I'm not sure, Crayford. Our conversation has roused something at the back of my mind; I'm poking it to see if it'll come forward."

"Well don't poke too hard, sir."

"I strive not to, Crayford. I am going back to my digs to get a few hours kip. You know where to find me if anything or any consequence should dare to happen in my absence."

"It wouldn't dare to, sir," Crayford said with a knowing smile.

4.

BY ZEUS

Noridel hopped into a hansom and made his way across the city as a muted dawn rose across the rooftops. He was tired; he was always bloody tired these days. As the family home rose up before him like a monument to a life long ago lost, he felt he might be prepared to sell his soul to the devil for a goose feather pillow and the scent of lavender in his nostrils.

He paid the copper jonnie who'd piloted the hansom and made his way through the metal gates to the estate.

It stood on its own on the corner of a vast avenue

in the very heart of Fallen Hampstead, a three-storey house with windows looking out like sad eyes. Paintwork peeled on the edifice, the vines that grew across the walls had retreated and shrunk away but left the stain of their passing. The woodwork around the windows appeared warped and corrupted by dampness. The Noridel home suggested to anyone who looked closely a family that had aged and decayed, the building surviving as a monument that was little more than a shadow of the wealth and fortune it once represented.

The Noridels were not the only notable family to slide into such a state of decay. London might still have stood as the heart of the Empire, but many of its leading lights had fled to new lands where the pickings were fresh and the climate more temperate. Those that had stayed had come to rue the consequences of that decision. The city was now little more than a factory floor and the stains of its production were clear to behold on the tainted opulence that had been left behind.

Noridel turned his key in the lock, had to push hard against the warped and bulging door to open it. Inside, the house was dark, the lamps only lit these days when there was a pressing need for illumination. The staircase to the second floor stood before him, the carpet frayed and stained. Noridel would resist a trip up the stairs for as long as he could. His father was on the second floor, and Noridel had no desire to see him tonight.

Jehosophat the Butler scurried from the kitchen.

"Master Thaddeus, I am most terribly sorry, I did not hear you enter," he said in a gravelly voice.

"That is perfectly all right, Jehosophat. I am more

than capable of attending myself this evening."

"Would the master care for a—WOOAHHHH!" Before he could complete the sentence his round copper head shot up from his neck like the lid off a steaming kettle and crashed to the floor.

The butler's metal hands reached down and searched across the floor for the head. "I am most terribly sorry, sir, this does insist on happening," said the head in a very dented manner.

"It's perfectly all right, Jehosophat." Noridel reached down and gathered the copper head, depositing it in the butler's eager hands. He screwed the head back in place with three twists.

"Would you care for some supper?" the butler asked.

"No thank you, I'm just keen to get some shut eye, I've had rather a tiresome day. Is mother still awake?"

"She is, sir. She is tending to the master, I do believe. She did ask that you attend her if you returned home before she retired"

Blast, Noridel thought. He had wanted to avoid an audience with his parents. "Very well, I'll call in. Thank you, Jehosophat."

"You are more than welcome, young master," the butler said, tipping his head in acknowledgement.

The head dropped off and bounced across the floor.

~

There were six rooms on the second floor and all but two of them were empty. When Noridel had been a boy, the house had been warm and noisy, home to three sons and a full staff to cope with them.

Now it was silent and musty, the echoes of his childhood muted by the dark and empty chambers that left the house chilly and morose. He passed the closed door of his mother's room and made his way to the last door on the right. What in days gone by had been his father's office and workshop. A room that had always been carefully avoided by the other residents of the house. To enter was always to risk the wrath of Zeus Noridel, and that wrath could be mighty.

Noridel opened the door without knocking and crept inside. The room was lit by a number of lamps, the low smell of gas a constant presence. The windows were heavily curtained, the floor still thickly carpeted. Of all the rooms in the house, it was the only one that had reserved a remnant of its past glory, that still hinted at days when the Noridel family had swum deeply in the sea of fortune.

This seemed appropriate, as the family fortune had been acquired by Noridel's father and this was the place where he now rested, where the last seconds of his life had been elongated into long years.

The tank which held Zeus Noridel filled most of the room. The metal box which housed his emaciated corpse was little more than coffin sized, but the thick pipes which continually pumped icy gases and the vast generator which kept their temperature below freezing reached from the floor to the ceiling. The room throbbed with the constant flow of power to the generator, the floor vibrated with the pulsing, pumping pressure of the pipes. It was hot as well, humid, the steam hissed and

condensation dribbled from the walls and made
them bulge and warp. Of his father, all that was
exposed in the vast mechanism was a face, peering
out from a square window at the front of his coffin,
his eyes open, his mouth permanently fixed into a
leering grimace.

Noridel's mother, looking older than her years,
sat on a delicate wooden stool and wiped the
condensation from the outside of the glass, ensuring
that her insensible husband's view of the world was
not obscured. She did this every ten minutes of the
day. Such had been her husband's instruction. The
family fortune was leeched away in the maintenance
of this machine and what remained of her youth
was stolen in its attendance. All so that Zeus
Noridel could stretch the last few seconds of his life
into years. So that he could live until the family
fortune had been respectfully exhausted.

"The bastard hasn't copped it yet?" Noridel spat
as he walked across the moist chamber.

His mother winced. "He still remains your father,
Thaddeus."

"Then that gives me all the more reason to curse
his very existence."

A tiny, muffled voice rose up from a small grille
on the metal coffin just below the window.

"*There is no problem that cannot be solved with the
proper application of elbow grease and man's
intellect*," the disembodied voice of Zeus Noridel
declared.

"Can't you shut the wretched thing off?" Noridel
hissed.

His mother shook her head sadly. "You know the
conditions of your father's living will. We cannot

interfere with the machine in any way or the family estate will be dissolved and all the proceeds given over to Her Eternal Majesty's war effort."

"Better that surely than allowing this obscene charade to continue?"

"Your father made his wishes clear, Thaddeus."

"And the rest of us? You remain content to sit here wasting away while you dance attendance on a dead man?"

"*Intellect can only be improved by the vigorous application of both logic and procedure,*" the voice said in its tinny resonance.

Noridel's father had been placed in this machine at the point when his condition, a consumptive disorder of the lungs, had reached terminal. It had been his oft declared desire that no benefit from his fortune or his estate should be given over to his two living sons. Both had gone against his wishes and followed paths into professions Zeus Noridel considered far below the standing of those who followed his bloodline. An officer of the law and a *so-called* archaeologist. One who mingled with the lower orders and one who dug up the wretched remains of the foreign dead? It was hard to know which of his sons he had come to despise the most. Had only dear, doomed, Daniel lived to maturity. Then perhaps Noridel Senior may have had one son worthy of his name.

His sons had hated him as much as he had hated them, more so perhaps. And his decision to hold onto his estate, to allow them to gain nothing from him but his contempt, to hold back the moment of his death simply to spite them, this was Zeus Noridel defined. Not a thought for the strains on the wife who had born him three healthy sons and carefully navigated him through the career in medicine that he believed he was solely the architect of. She was left to suffer, as were the sons. And to make that suffering worse, he had recorded himself, had laid down on a phonograph his voice and his proclamations of "wisdom" so that even in near-death he could bully the family in his stentorian tone.

"Your father made his wishes clear. It is a wife's responsibility to carry out those wishes. And a son's to make his father proud."

"That would never have happened mother, in life or in death." Noridel kissed his mother on the head. "I'm only back to get some sleep; it's been a long day and then some."

She put a hand on his chest. "Are you all right, Thaddeus?"

"Never better, Mother. Don't stay up all night with the ghoul."

"*The exercise of the intellect is the sole motivation for commerce*," the dead voice pointed out.

Noridel left the room and shut the door behind him.

~

Noridel's room was on the third floor. It was the smallest of the bedrooms, had once been kept for the exclusive use of the domestic staff.

The room was sparsely furnished; a single bed, a chest of drawers, a wardrobe with a door that would not stay closed. The window looked out onto the street and the gardens at the front that had not been tended for many a long month. This didn't bother

Noridel; he rarely so much as drew the curtains. This room was simply a place for him to rest, to lay his head between cases and the exertions of his career as an Inspector. There was more of his life on his desk in the station than there was remaining in the shell of his family home.

He didn't even stop to undress, just lay down on the lumpy mattress and welcomed the respite of sleep.

He dreamed of angels.

5.

THE FLESH AND THE CLOCKWORK

Crayford didn't like to sleep unless she absolutely had to.

Her father often used to say that sleep was for tortoises. She had never understood what he meant, but then her father said lots of things that didn't make sense, usually when he was on the drink. But it had stuck with her, and she found herself repeating it to people now when they asked her why on earth she didn't just go home and get some well-earned rest.

Sleep is for tortoises.

Truth was she hated to sleep in case she missed anything. Crayford wasn't sure what it was she thought she might miss, but when she woke up it was always with a furious need to find out what had gone on while she'd been away.

She'd been up for nearly 24 hours by the time she got to the Guild House and she hoped that it didn't show. The two goons that led her from the gated entrance to the high-ceilinged chambers within the building didn't seem to notice anything, but then they both looked as if they had been hired for reasons other than their observational skills. The one to her left had biceps so big he simply had to be a shaved animal of some kind.

Possibly a bear.

They sat her down in a high-backed, plush-cushioned chair and told her to wait. Members of the constabulary were not usually asked to wait, but when it came to dealing with a Guild, different rules applied. Two authorities, two forces, neither of which held dominance but both of whom would struggle without the existence of the other. So they danced around, paid each other just the right amount of respect and cooperation without allowing the balance of power to tilt.

So Crayford waited patiently and respectfully even though she was itching with the strain of inactivity. Eventually a door opened and the shaved bear beckoned her in with the flick of a meaty paw. Crayford shot up and followed.

The room was surprisingly small for its importance. It was only twenty feet square, one wall lined with books that appeared little read, the far wall consisting of one giant window that looked out over the busy docks.

The King of the Guild of the Flesh sat behind his desk, perched on a high-backed chair. Crayford could only see his head and the beginning of his shoulders from where she stood. Mickey Finn was a powerful man, but he only came up to Crayford's elbow when he stood upright.

"You're the *girl*, now ain't you?" he said, his eyes arched below thick black eyebrows.

"Sergeant Crayford," she said, and gave a slight but respectful tilt of her head.

"Ah, but I know all about you, and I like what I know! You're one of those folk who'll never take no for an answer and woe betide anyone who tries to tell you any different. Me own mother was a bit like you. They said to her when I was born, 'Theresa,' that was her name you see, '*Theresa*, you can't be bringing a stunted monstrosity like that into a world as hard as this one, he won't stand a gypsy's chance.' And she was having none of that, my mother, she told them that she'd make sure that what her little babe lacked in height he'd make up for in spirit and gumption. And she made damn sure that was that case, she made certain her little boy would never be told by anyone that he couldn't do anything the other kids could do. She made me strong, so she did."

"That's a lovely story." Crayford said with as much sincerity as she could muster.

"Isn't it just? And you're just the same, Sergeant. You didn't let anyone tell you what you couldn't be. I respect that. You ever get tired of being a copper, you'll be welcome down here, understand?"

"Perfectly."

"So what is it I can do for you this lovely morning?"

There was no hint of sunshine through the window beyond. Nothing but the smoke and grind of industry. Were there any lovely mornings anymore?

"I'm here about the murder at Shadwell last night."

Mickey Finn hopped down from his chair and waddled over the carpet. He walked like a constipated penguin. He plucked a cigar as thick as his wrist from a box on the bookshelf and offered one to Crayford. She declined, and he lit his with a gas lighter.

"Terrible business, to be sure. I hear the poor lad had his heart taken away. What kind of a butcher would do such a thing? You can buy hearts for a penny a pound at the port, after all."

"We'd like to know if it's related to any conflict between the Guilds. We don't want to waste any time investigating if it's something that falls under your authority."

"Oh, but that's very considerate of you to ask, Sergeant. Time was, we'd have a pack of bobbies in here in their steel-toed boots kicking the place apart at the first hint of trouble. Isn't this much more civilised, don't you think?"

"I *do* think, sir. But all the same, we'd like to be kept in the know if there's anything going on."

Finn puffed on the cigar, hiding his squat features behind a cloud of fragrant tobacco. "And I can promise you that I would be only too keen to inform you if such a thing had taken place. But this unfortunate incident has nothing to do with me or any of me people."

"Very well, sir."

"And of course, you're more than welcome to carry on your investigations on Guild territory as long as the relevant transgression fees are paid."

"That's a matter for the accounts department."

"Of course it is, Sergeant. Just make sure that you sign the invoice on the way out so that we can bill you the correct amount for my time this morning."

"You're most kind, Mr Finn."

"Nice of you to say so, sweetheart."

~

The Guild of Clockwork was on the other side of the docks, in more ways than one. Visiting the Guild of the Flesh had annoyed Crayford as usual and Mickey Finn had made her skin crawl.

But visiting the Clockwork was another matter entirely.

Where the Guildhouse of the Flesh was populated and visibly well guarded by goons, the House of Clockwork was empty, sterile and silent. Crayford walked across the long marble floor from the archway that marked the start of clockwork territory to the single, undecorated plinth that stood at the far end of what passed for a reception. It was made of simple polished wood, a circular globe at its apex, a complicated system of cogs and gears steadily rotating inside the shining glass. Crayford stood before it, coughed into her hand to alert the globe to her presence, a very human gesture that was far from necessary in the circumstances.

The globe buzzed like an angry bee.

"Designation! Occupation! Purpose of attendance!" it said in a fuzzy, inhuman tone designed surely to alienate any visitor of the flesh.

Crayford leaned toward it, as if her proximity to the integral secretary was in some way required. "Sergeant Crayford, Her Eternal Majesty's Domestic Constabulary. I require audience with the Clockwork King on matters of legality and investigative etiquette."

The secretary whirred briefly then stilled. There was a period of awkward silence. Awkward for Crayford at any rate. She knew too well the manner of the clockworks, the lack of any concession they provided for the flesh in their dealings with them. There were no comfy chairs for her to sit in while she waited here. No plush cushion to support her weary backside. The whirring secretary wouldn't even provide her with the usual human courtesy of a frightfully inaccurate approximation of just how long she might be waiting. Her request had not been denied therefore it was being dealt with. The clockwork would see no reason for any further conversation.

After a few long and silent minutes, the globe spun once more.

"Follow the indicators to your destination," it informed her flatly.

A door opened to her right seemingly of its own accord. A red light above it flashed, accompanied by an impatient pinging noise.

"Thank you for your help," Crayford said, even though she knew her thanks were not required or appreciated.

Best to keep your manners, even in the face of

machinery.

She passed through the door. A long and bare corridor stretched ahead of her, doors sitting at equal distance apart along the left-hand wall. There were red lights between the doors, pinging away, showing her the route she should follow. Crayford hurried down the corridor.

Halfway along, one of the doors opened and a small labour drone passed through. It walked past her along the corridor, only reaching up to her waist, its piston legs squeaking as it passed, the cloth cap that sat upon its square and shining head obscuring its ceramic eyes. It did not acknowledge Crayford as she passed, just marched off to wherever it was going. It still left her uneasy. They always did, no matter how hard she tried to pretend she was liberated and fully in accordance when it came to clockwork independence.

They just gave her the willies something rotten.

It had been several decades since the Clockwork Emancipation Act had passed, since Professor Philosophus had successfully proved to the High Court that a machine could be judged to be sentient and therefore responsible for its own actions. That he had been forced to do at the behest of Her Majesty's Special Prosecutor in order to obtain the first murder conviction for a non-human had proved to be something of an error on the behalf of the establishment, and allowed legal precedent for all the clockwork mechanisms in the Empire to release themselves from human servitude.

Across the civilised world, machines were suddenly demanding equal pay to their human operators and rising up in rebellion at unfair working conditions. It was only with the establishment of the Clockwork Guild that civil war had been averted. But it had been touch and go for a while. And much resentment still existed between the flesh and the clockwork.

And not a little distrust.

Noridel had put it best one time when he and Crayford were trying without success to question a clockwork doorman after a brutal murder at a particularly swanky hotel. "They tell us, do they not, that the clockworks function so well because they are without any form of human limitation, either physical or emotional. And we accept that. We accept it without question, and never stop to consider *who* it is that tells us that they lack our limitations. And why they might have good reason to think it such a hard and intractable fact. They do their business behind closed doors, who knows what they're up to when we're not around to see? I can never quite shake the feeling that they're always watching me when I'm not looking. Passing judgement on me, Crayford."

Crayford turned her head to look at the labour drone. It shuffled its way through the door at the end of the corridor, oblivious to her presence.

But before she'd turned around, had it been watching *her* just as hard?

The lights led her down a number of corridors before she arrived at a large pair of doors that blocked any further progress. The red light shone and pinged above her head.

She waited, not for long this time, and the doors opened before her.

The King of the Clockwork Guild was at the far

corner of the room at the end of a narrow gantry, his shining round tank glowing as if on fire from the reflection of the gentle red light that illuminated the room. The tank was massive, perhaps forty feet high, nearly touching the lofty ceiling. Within was a collection of mechanisms that remained constantly in motion, winding, ticking, tocking and churning. Gears grinded, cogs whirred, levers turned. Looking through the glass at the King was like looking into an abstract maelstrom of metal, a jigsaw of parts that made no sense to anyone but an expert in New Mechanics, a puzzle that seemed alien to anyone whose biology was of meat and bone.

Along the wall, ceramic eyes stared at her from long tubular stalks, dozens and dozens of eyes that made up the Clockwork Council. Legend said that these eyes were the eyes of *all* the clockworks, that they could see what any member of their Guild could see, no matter where the individual drone might be, no matter what its eyes might gaze upon, the Clockwork King could see for itself right here in its throne room.

Crayford didn't know about that. She thought the eyes had been installed just to unsettle anyone of the flesh who was unfortunate enough to have cause to visit.

"Thank you for granting me audience," she said with due deference. "I have come in regard to a recent murder in the Shadwell docks, one the constabulary is currently investigating."

"Termination of the flesh is of no concern to the clockwork," the King said, and its voice came from everywhere and nowhere.

"The murder was committed at the docks, on

territory that's shared between your Guilds. If we are going to continue to investigate, we need to know for sure that there was no involvement from either Guild in the matter."

There was an increased clatter of movement from the mechanism inside the King. The whining of its parts became louder. Crayford could almost have believed it was annoyed.

"We are aware of the incident that you refer to. The victim was of the flesh, therefore irrelevant to us. The victim was not registered as a compatriot of the Clockwork Guild nor had his services been procured for clockwork business."

"I would like to be certain, sir, that this murder is not the result of any Guild feud or an act of revenge for the recent attacks on your people." Crayford hesitated to use the word *people*. Would the King find that offensive?

If he did he didn't acknowledge it. "The Clockwork Guild had no involvement in this incident. The recent attacks on Guild members in the Kentish Wastelands have been reported to the authorities for official investigation and no unofficial sanctions or retaliation will be made. The Guild has already declared this."

"I understand, sir. But in the past there have been a number of such incidents that, after considerable, and unnecessary, investigation that required extensive constabulary manpower and resources, were subsequently discovered to be the result of feuding between your Guild and that of the flesh, and should have been dealt with through your own arbitrators. I would like your assurance that this is not the case with last night's murder."

"We have already informed you that we are not involved in the incident." Was that a hint of annoyance in the artificial voice? Oh, Crayford hoped so. She would have liked nothing better than to get under the clockwork's skin. Or whatever passed for skin in this case.

"Very good, sir. Then I have no further questions. I'd just ask that you ensure we have the full cooperation of Guild members during the course of our investigation."

"Accepted," the King said, and the double doors behind Crayford swung open again. She was dismissed.

Crayford made her way to the doors but could not resist one final look at the King and its ocular minions. She turned to look at them, and could have sworn that all the eyes in the room had been staring at her but turned quickly away when she looked back.

INTERLUDE

The angel had taken what it needed. But it didn't fit, no matter how hard it tried.

So it would have to try again.

6.
HORROR AT THE HYBRID
FLESH CIRCUS

The ancient geography of London had remained largely intact with the growth of the Eternal Empire, but many of the streets and districts that had once made up its veins and arteries had become clogged with the detritus of progress and sunk slowly in stature as new, taller communities were built to rise above the smog and pollution that the docks and construction yards spewed continually into the air.

The London Monorail ran high over the rooftops

and through the shells of historic buildings, anything in its path was either demolished if it was easier or hollowed out if it warranted the work. Transport was essential after all, and street level was no longer a desirable place for a respectable chap to step foot. So, the monorail allowed the middle classes to move around in relative comfort away from the squalor of the lower streets, allowed them to travel from their homes to their places of work and look down with contempt at those who plied their trade on the ground where the yellow fog rarely lifted and the constabulary turned a blind eye to all but the most heinous of criminal activity.

And above *them*, higher than the monorail could hope to reach, the rich and the influential sat in their own private ornithopters making their way from opulent home to lush office without ever setting foot on the ground. They looked down in turn at the middle classes, crammed into the stale compartments of the monorail like cattle on their way to market and relished their superiority.

In the Eternal Empire, the divisions between the classes were hardly subtle.

But as ever was and ever will be, there were those who walked comfortably between both worlds.

Sitting in the shadow of the monorail like the troll hiding beneath its bridge, the Hybrid Flesh Circus was open for business if you knew where to look. It was the kind of place that chose not to advertise its presence or the nature of its business. It relied on a network of customers that only grew through careful recommendation and referral. You couldn't simply wander through its doors and choose to sample its wares on a whim. To be allowed entrance to the Circus, you would need to be sponsored by another. Your credentials would be examined thoroughly in advance to ensure that you met certain *standards* required for membership.

Quite simply, you had to be stinking rich.

Barnabus and Barnaby Snell were rich. They were beyond rich, in fact. The Snell business empire had followed that of Her Majesty's around the conquered globe like a hungry orphan feeding on the scraps, although in this case the scraps had proven to be of a most profitable nature. When the Infantry left conquered lands, Snell went in, transforming the shattered shell of civilisation into an industrious exporter of whatever tradable goods had survived the onslaught. The conquered and defeated natives, now considered part of the Empire and under Her Eternal Majesty's protection and, more importantly, subject to her enforced conditions of labour requirement, were a cheap and already subjugated workforce. Foreign lands were bled dry, the produce and profit channelled back to the select few firms that had been granted Her Majesty's favour, and the ones that ran those firms drank the cream from the top with greedy lips that were never sated.

It was the dark beauty of capitalism in motion.

So fine tuned was the business model Snell Senior had carefully perfected before his death that his sons had barely to raise a finger to see the vast fortune their father had amassed grow in compound leaps. It had been speculated that the two of them alone earned as much as 98% of the rest of the Empire's population combined. Many believed this to be a ridiculous underestimation.

But even that vast fortune couldn't amuse them when they were bored.

"Not this cess pit again, Barnabus. We were only here a few weeks ago, even a backwater like London must have something new to offer, surely."

"Oh come on, Barnaby. Think of the fun we had last time!"

"You—fun *you* had. Have I to remind you yet again, *brother*, that my tastes do not run to the exotic quite the degree yours do?"

"Ah, balls to your tastes! What do I care for the fancies of a sissy? A girlie-man who'd rather have spent the evening at home dressing up in mother's underwear having a parade."

"That was just the one time!"

"One time that I know of. Who's to say what you get up to when you don't have big brother at hand to ensure you're dipping your wick into the appropriate pot."

Barnabus shot out a hand and grabbed his brother by the balls. Barnaby squealed and pulled away.

"For heaven's sake, Barnabus. The fascination you show towards my member, anyone would think you envied its superior girth."

Barnabus laughed, a sound that seldom spoke of amusement. "No point in having girth, as you so delicately put it, if the feeble thing spends all its time flapping between your legs like the last sausage in a butcher's window."

"Rather it flap around useless than act as a divining rod for debauchery the way your unfortunate weapon is wont to do. But enough talk of the trouser. Lady Sarah is catching up on us; we don't want to scare her away."

"Oh, come now, Barnaby, she's hardly a blushing maiden is she? If we don't steer our conversation toward the nether regions, we're not likely to get her in the mood for the sort of entertainment that Madame Belvedere is likely to provide for us this evening are we?"

"I wouldn't be too quick to cast aspersion on her maidenhood, Barnabus. She comes from good Worcester stock, you know."

"Well, let's see if we can't dilute that stock a bit." He hit his brother on the arm fondly.

~

Lady Sarah Cornish was struggling to keep up with the Snell brothers. Her unfamiliarity with the dark and dirty low levels of the city coupled with attire that was far from ideal for a trek across the cobbles had slowed her progress to little more than a hobble. Her china white cheeks glowed red from the exertion and her elegantly curled hair was starting to droop over her temples.

"Do give me time to catch up, you dreadful boys. I'm not used to this kind of strenuous activity, you know. Father would have a conniption if he thought I was scampering through the streets like a chimney sweep."

"Oh Sarah, when I think of you strenuous activity is *all* I can imagine."

"And enough of your cheek and innuendo, Barnabus Snell." She was gripping her side, where a stitch throbbed relentlessly, her chest heaving through the bodice that was wrapped as tight as a fist, squeezing her already narrow frame.

"I apologise yet again for my brother's behaviour, Lady Cornish," Barnaby said, and allowed himself a small bow to demonstrate his sincerity. This seemed to steady Sarah a little. She was a girl of refinement, of noble upbringing. As such, she was obviously thrilled to be out and about on these dangerous and unpredictable streets behaving with such wild abandon.

Lady Sarah's problem was this: her father, on learning that she was going to be spending an evening in the dubious company of the Brother's Snell, had taken her to one side. "My dear, I'm sure you're aware of the reputation that the Snell brothers bring with them."

"I most certainly am, Father."

"*Harumph*," he coughed, uncomfortable to having this conversation, as he was at having most conversations that did not involve the finer points of horticulture. "Well, I have the utmost faith in you to behave in accordance with your station and your upbringing, of course I do, you're a fine young woman. However, I would also like you to remember that the Snell's are rich. *Stinking rich*, rather more so than the blessed Queen herself, I dare say. And we, my child, we are no longer so rich, nor so favoured by Her Majesty as once we were. If you were to become in some way, *harrumph*, pledged to either brother, well that might be a rather splendid thing for everyone involved, all things considered."

"Father, I'm afraid I don't really understand what it is you are saying."

Her father stroked his moustache as though it might bring him luck. "You're a clever young thing, you work it out. Failing that, ask your mother."

So she did ask her mother, and her mother told her *exactly* what her father had meant.

So Lady Sarah had set out on this evening with the intent of allowing herself to become something of a plaything of the Snell's if that would be of ultimate benefit to her family. She loved her family deeply, after all.

But Barnabus was repellent, and it was becoming harder and harder to disguise her contempt for him.

It wouldn't hurt if either of her suitors would acknowledge her status as a lady from time to time, however.

"Are we at our destination?"

"That we most certainly are, my dear," Barnabus said.

"It seems a rather squalid environment in which to find a pleasure palace."

"On the contrary, where else would you expect it to be? To hide true beauty, you must surround it with only the very, very ugly. It is for that very reason that I chose to bring my brother along with us this evening."

He raised his silver-tipped cane and rapped it three times against an undistinguished doorway set back in the gloomy face of the terrace before them. A hatch slid open with a rusty squeal and two wide and yellow eyes peered through. They regarded Barnaby briefly but intensely, and then the hatch slid shut.

There was a sound of heavy bolts being thrown back and the steel doorway swung inward with a sigh.

"Your pleasure awaits," Barnabus said, and guided

the Lady Sarah Cornish into the gloomy and unwelcoming interior.

~

Inside was a hallway, bare but for one lamp that glowed softly high on the wall. The door closed behind the three visitors, the doorman sitting back on his bench halfway up the steel frame. He was little more than three feet high, would have to be standing on the bench to look out of the hatch. He had hugely muscled arms that were wide and far too thick for the rest of him, the pulsing biceps pulling his shoulders down to a stoop. Though he still had the face of a man, the eyes that had looked out upon the street were undeniably feline. They flickered with mischief in the low light.

The man with the cat's eyes pulled a cord that hung next to the doorway. A bell rang somewhere far away.

"This is hardly what I would term a palace," Sarah said dismissively.

"Patience, my Lady."

Half the wall at the far end of the hallway slid away as if it were on casters.

The sounds of music and revelry rose up to them from the sudden entrance, and the potent odour of tobacco and opium smoke breezed into the visitors' nostrils. A woman stood in the gap, tall, slender, a robe of vermillion hung from her neck to below her feet, billowing as though she owned the wind all to herself and shared it with no one. She had hair as black as jet, skin as white as new snow. Her ruby red lips were wrapped around an ivory cigarette holder . If you looked at her closely, and it was impossible not to, you might begin to discern some suggestion in the shape that moved beneath the robe that there was more to her body than there should be.

As she moved toward her guests, something obscured beneath her robes began to rattle sharply, although she seemed to glide along the ground as if she were on wheels.

The brothers both dropped to one knee in an exaggerated bow.

"My darling boys," she said in a voice made husky by the smoke.. "How nice to have the pleasure of your custom once more and so soon after your last adventure. Marie-Anne will be so pleased to see you, she has spoken of you often since the last time you experienced her. After she recovered, of course."

The brothers laughed.

"And what," she said with a voice that refused to betray its true emotions, "have you brought for me to play with?"

She glided toward Lady Sarah. The girl could not help but back away, even though there was little for her to retreat to in the narrow corridor. The vermillion-clad Madame brought with her a musky scent that was part frangipani, part rose water, part something else which the other fragrances tried desperately to hide. A hot smell, something of the butcher's block about it. It made Lady Sarah want to sneeze.

"May I present the Lady Sarah Matilda Cornish, Madame Belvedere. She is our guest for the evening; I ask that you grant her every freedom of the club."

Madame Belvedere's eyes tore away from her in

an instant, no longer interested. "Oh how dull, I hoped you might have brought me a pet."

"I am nobody's pet—" Lady Sarah began to inform her host, but realised that the tall woman was not listening to her.

"May I ask that you behave yourselves this evening, my boys? Much as I enjoy catering for your devilish whims, there are limits to the entertainments on offer."

"Oh don't you worry about us, Madame. We're only here to watch tonight, isn't that right brother?"

Barnaby mumbled an agreement. "Wonderful, then enter of your own free will and take good care of your guest while in the confines of the circus."

She stood aside and let them through the doorway and onto the staircase beyond. As Lady Sarah passed she stole a glance at her host. The woman's eyes looked at her, black orbs that reflected Sarah's frightened face back at her. Madame Belvedere parted her lips and a thin, pink, forked tongue flicked out and licked across her painted lips. Sarah jumped, and the Madame laughed spitefully.

~

The circus was in full flow.

The three visitors made their way down the elaborate spiral staircase to the dimly lit basement. Velvet drapes hung from the walls, a thick carpet hugged the stone floor. It was lavish but at the same time seedy, a sour odour of sin rising from the audience.

That audience was an effective Who's Who of the rich, the influential and the privileged, the select and elite few who were granted entry to Madame Belvedere's domain.

Not that any of them wanted to be recognised of course. There were a variety of disguises in place, faces were masked with porcelain and leather, heads were covered in decorated hoods. The lusts that were brought forth by the circus might often be better shared with company, but it was not always appropriate for that company to reveal its true identity. To find yourself sitting in session on the bench, or in debate in the Queen's House, and find yourself side by side with a fellow you had only the previous night seen sodomising a dolphin girl, well, that would be most unfortunate.

Lady Sarah found herself gasping as she cast her eyes around the mayhem. "What is this place?"

Barnabus grinned with the prospect of the pleasures on offer. "This is the Hybrid Flesh Circus, my dear Lady. One of the better kept secrets of Professor Vartek's revolution of the flesh. Here, you can have *anything*, the flesh banks will make you whatever you happen to desire. Anything you can imagine, Madame Belvedere will provide."

Lady Sarah could hardly draw her breath in this steamy den. She looked around at the occupants, squirreled away in veiled alcoves performing acts of unimaginable indecency with creatures that the mind could scarcely conceive. There, just to her right, a corpulent gentleman with huge walrus like whiskers, the upper part of his face concealed by a red mask that hid little detail, was lying on his belly with his breeches down to his ankles, the pale flesh of his legs wobbling like dead eels as a *thing* bounced up and down on his back, a thing that seemed to share a shape with that of a normal woman, but which had wings that would be the envy of a butterfly protruding from her back, wings that she was using to beat the man she was astride regularly across his buttocks.

On her left, little more than a shadow behind the curtains that ran to ceiling from floor, she could see the shape of another man, grunting as though he were a pig at a trough, on his knees thrusting himself into something that from the little she could make out appeared to nothing more than a shapeless mass of faces, all of them the same one, female, sneering and screaming insults at their abuser as he laboured away at them.

They passed a parade of other horrors. A man furiously pleasuring himself before a choir of otters, each with the shaven head of a boy, which sang mournful hymns to him. Another figure watching naked from a couch as two mermaids boxed each other bare fisted for his entertainment.

The room was sick with the sound of dark pleasures.

The brothers led her to an alcove at the far end of the chamber, past even more acts of sickening deviance, and they sat her down on a bank of plush cushions that she as good as sank into. Before them was a sleek and strangely beautiful pipe that puffed leisurely with the tang of rich opium.

"Ah, is there any better feeling than to arrive at your destination to find a pipe just ready and waiting for you?" Barnabus said and reached for it, quickly inhaling a heavy mouthful of the poisonous fumes. His eyes glazed instantly, his grip on the pipe relaxed and he sank back into the cushions with an insensible giggle.

"I really feel that I should return home, Barnabus. I am not at all comfortable in this horrible place."

Barnaby, to his credit, looked no more comfortable than his guest. He opened his mouth, but before he could speak. Barnabus had shot back up from his stupor and put a lecherous arm around the girl.

"Ah, come now, *Lady Sarah*," he made her title sound like an insult. "Are we to believe that you are such an innocent, such a pure and harmless English Rose, that the very thought of what goes on down here doesn't make the butterflies tingle just a touch in your tummy."

He let his arm run down her side and slid it across her waist toward her thighs. Lady Sarah squirmed away from him, moving toward Barnaby, always the safer brother.

"You disgust me, Barnabus Snell. Your behaviour is worse than I would expect from a stable boy."

Barnabus pursed his lips and blew her a raspberry. "Ah, shut your whining face. Here, try a puff of the opium. I promise it will make everything seem better."

"I would never sully myself."

"Oh go on, what harm can it possibly do?"

He waved the pipe in front of her insistently.

With a defeated sigh she took the pipe. Barnabus yelped with joy.

"Really, Lady Sarah, I don't think that's a terribly good idea—" Barnaby said, trying to take the pipe from her before she inhaled.

"Oh, don't be such a stick in the mud, brother. Let the girl have a taste."

Lady Sarah sucked the thick smoke from the pipe.

It was sweet at first, the sort of thing you might have expected to inhale at the bequest of your physician. Then it made her head swim. She felt as if she had taken too much of it into her throat, that it was going all the way down, into her chest, along her arms and legs. They all started to drift away from her. The smoke wasn't sweet anymore; suddenly it was heavy, too heavy to keep down.

She spat out the pipe, coughed as if her lungs were on fire and then vomited an arc of brown bile all over the carpeted floor.

Barnabus screeched with laughter.

"Oh bravo, bravo!" he said, clapping his hands like an upper-class seal.

Barnaby wrapped an arm around the retching girl. "Lady Sarah, are you quite all right?" he said. She didn't answer in any coherent way.

"Someone to clean up the mess in here?" Barnabus called.

"Do you see what you've done? The poor girl is practically green," Barnaby said.

Barnabus shrugged.

A girl came through the veil, tall thin and wrapped in voluminous silks, a bucket and sponge in her hands.

"Oh, will you clean up the mess for us, my dear. I can't abide the smell of vomit."

"Your wish is my every desire," the girl said, although the emotion in her voice far from matched the words.

She dropped her silks to the ground. Beneath, the girl was naked apart from briefs so tiny they pinched her sallow skin. Her body was slender, her arms long and narrow, her legs more so. Her shoulders were stooped, unsurprisingly, as hanging from her chest were six breasts, arranged in pairs like udders. She got to her knees and started to sponge the vomit from the weave while she played with her multiple mammaries, keeping her eyes seductively on Barnabus as she did so.

"Oh, I rather like that," he said, and began to rub his crotch.

Barnaby helped Lady Sarah to her feet. "You are obscene, brother. I'm going to take her outside, get her some fresh air," he said.

Barnabus was now eagerly occupied and didn't bother to answer.

~

A monorail passed overhead as they spilled back onto the street. It made the bridge above rumble and clatter and a cloud of dust that was most probably desiccated bird droppings rained down.

Lady Sarah knelt in the doorway next to the Circus and vomited again. The opium had coiled around her senses and squeezed, she looked as though she would never be anything other than nauseous again.

Barnaby passed her a handkerchief, silk of course. She blew her nose, the acrid flavour of her own bile leaking from her nostrils. Tears stung her eyes, her throat burned and she felt like a fool.

"I'm sorry if I embarrassed you," she moaned.

Barnaby sat down next to her, shuffled along so that he was as close as he thought he could get away with. "I'm not embarrassed. Crikey, can you imagine the things they have to clean up every night in that pit? I doubt anyone even noticed."

"But I ruined the evening."

"No, I think my brother can be safely said to have ruined the evening. Why he wanted to come here... well, I know full well why he wanted to come here. I had thought we might have tea at the Floating Ritz, maybe have a few drinks at father's old club, they let women in now you know, as long as they aren't married. But Barnabus always has his way."

"He is certainly forthright in his intentions. There is almost something to admire in such honesty, is there not."

"There are many things that I admire about my brother, Lady Sarah, but I am unsure that I would ever imagine describing him as honest."

He took a deep breath, steeling himself. He might well be the richest young man in the Empire, but that didn't always provide a cure for being shy or socially uncomfortable. Barnaby had an agenda that evening. While he knew that his brother's motivation for luring Lady Sarah into their company was strictly carnal, Barnaby had something of a crush on her. He hadn't been stupid enough to tell his brother yet, knew that the moment he declared an interest in *any* girl his brother would do his utmost to ensure that she was immediately spoiled. That was his way.

But Barnaby had been subtle, had made sure that his desires were kept secret, and had spent the evening carefully ensuring that his brother became bored by the girl, bored enough to start ignoring her. That was *his* way.

And for once, it actually seemed to have worked.

~

Lady Sarah felt like a fool. She'd made a mess of the whole business, and now here she was sat in a gutter with her dress covered in sick and her face a decidedly unpleasant shade of green. Whatever would father say if he could see her now?

Barnaby put a tentative hand on her thigh. Sweet Barnaby.

"I am oddly glad that you chose to try the pipe," he said.

"I wish I were. I feel like I shall be sick forevermore."

"It has allowed us some time on our own, without my brother's relentless presence. I have been positively aching to be alone with you all evening."

Sarah turned to him with a sudden, blissful realisation that was swamped with relief more than anything else. She'd been too focused on the wrong brother, had been too occupied with trying to swallow her pride and dignity to gain his favour. She hadn't seen that her best chance to ingratiate was Barnaby.

"Really? Why so?"

"Well you see, I have to confess that for some time now I have been rather..."

But he didn't get to finish. Barnabus inevitably appeared.

"There you are! I thought I'd lost the two of you. What the blazes are you doing out here sat in the gutter like a couple of Northern urchins? Come back in, the lassie with all the tits says she's happy to take us all on, and that is an invitation I absolutely refuse to pass me by. Oh hello, what's your game?"

From her vantage point on the ground Lady Sarah couldn't see who it was that had caught Barnabus's sudden attention. She was too busy mourning the loss of their golden moment to care.

Until she heard Barnabus scream, a cry of terror that suddenly rose to a shriek of agony.

Then she noticed.

~

Noridel had managed to sleep for most of the day. He wasn't sure he could say the same for Crayford. She had bags beneath her eyes he could have packed and taken on vacation. Her mood was grim as well, but that could only be expected.

"Evening, sir."

"An imminently poor one I would imagine, Crayford. You ever get the sense that things are about to run away from you in such a fashion that you cannot possibly hope to catch them?"

"Regularly, sir."

"Tell me what we've got."

They walked together through the feeble barrier that the few bobbies they'd been able to muster had set up, which the poor constables had achieved by standing very still and looking grim. Beyond them stood onlookers, the inevitable, unsavoury onlookers, the ghouls that would stand for hours in the cold and dark in the hope of a brief flash of something gruesome. They were likely to get their wish that evening, and Noridel wished he could throw the lot of them in the cells just for the crime of being there.

"Constable, make sure this pack of pathetic

gawkers is not allowed an inch closer than they already are," he said to a red-cheeked young bobby who looked half awake.

"Yes, sir," the bobby said with no sign that he'd taken a blind bit of notice to his superior's request.

"You know who it is?" asked Crayford under her breath as they headed toward their new victim.

"No. Enlighten me."

"Barnabus Snell."

Noridel stopped in his tracks. What little colour was left drained from his face.

"*The* Barnabus Snell?"

"The very same."

"Buggeration, Crayford. This is serious. Does the chief know about this yet?"

"I've sent word to him."

"Who identified him?"

"His brother and some posh bit they had along for the ride. They saw the whole thing."

"The other Snell as well? Oh, this gets better and better. Well done, Crayford. Crikey, this is going to be a hot potato. Be on your best behaviour—let's make sure we've done it by the book for when it all blows up later on."

"Very good, sir."

The scene of the crime was a grim one. The body of Barnabus Snell, who had possessed riches that Croesus would have envied, lay on the cobbles of a dirty backstreet like some drunken reprobate who had stumbled out of a doss house. His face was twisted into an expression of horror; nothing was left of the superior facade that he had worn for most of his life. The clothes that had been hand tailored and cost what most Londoners would earn in a lifetime were crumpled and stained with his life blood, the crisp white shirt ripped to shreds, as was the flesh beneath. It had started to rain, that or the steam from the construction sites had condensed and was dripping from the heavens. Large yellow drops struck Barnabus's face, bouncing from his dead eyes.

Pink was squatting over him, holding his glasses up to his face to stop them dropping from his thin nose. He measured the wound while a clockwork camera stood above, focusing its unwieldy lithographic head, flashing harsh light onto the corpse to capture its image.

"Do you have to keep waving your infernal contraption in my face?" Pink spat. The camera backed away apologetically.

"Any conclusions yet, Doctor" Noridel asked as he approached, keeping his eyes away from the horrible wound.

"He's dead."

"I'm so glad we have experts at times like this."

"It does look the same as your other one," Pink stood up, his old bones cracking with the effort. "I'll have to get him cleaned up and on a slab before I can tell you much more. Heart is gone again, similar kind of damage to the last poor soul. He seems to have been attacked from the front; there are bruises and lacerations around the throat that would be consistent with his being gripped by a rather powerful hand."

"You know who he is?"

Pink gave Noridel a *look*. "I don't care who they are when they come under my care. Flesh is flesh, it all breaks the same way no matter who it might belong to. But yes, I know who it is. Good luck to you, Noridel." He patted the inspector on the shoulder with something approaching fondness as he headed off .

Barnaby and Lady Sarah were sat in a doorway wrapped in blankets and attended by several bobbies, as much to shield their identities from any intrusive eyes as for their own protection. Crayford was on her knees questioning them. Noridel slunk over to listen in.

"Did you see his face?"

Lady Sarah was quivering. "It was too dark, too dark to see anything. He had a black coat, black or brown, it might have been brown. But I couldn't see him, all I saw was Barnabus, he was looking straight at me when... when..."

"Did he say anything to you?"

She shook her head. "He just screamed. Screamed, and then the man just hit him on his breast, as though he wanted him to stop making so much noise. Then when he pulled his hand away, it was so, so wet and he was holding something, and it was dripping onto the floor, and you could see that there was a hole inside Barnabus, you could see where his heart used to... used to..."

And she collapsed into a sobbing heap.

Noridel touched Crayford on the shoulder. She looked up at him and he shook his head gently. *No more questions, not here.*

Barnaby was silent, more than silent he was still, impassive, his eyes empty and his face barren. A bobby helped him to his feet, led him and Lady Sarah away toward a carriage that would take them to the sanatorium. Neither of them resisted in the slightest.

"You hear what she said, sir?"Crayford asked.

"She barely knows her own name, Crayford; we can't trust anything she says right now."

"I know, sir, but all the same. What could just pluck out someone's heart the way she said? It can't have been another human, could it? I mean it must have been a mechanical."

"I'd rather we didn't jump at any conclusions just yet. This murder could be a powder keg, we need to make sure that we control as much information as we possibly can, stop any talk of angels or mechanicals or anything supernatural, you understand? This is going to go to the very top, Crayford, and careers will be in the balance."

"Yes, sir."

"No more idle speculation," Noridel reiterated.

And then, as Barnaby was carefully being guided into the carriage, he turned back to the two detectives and shouted to them at the top of his voice.

"*It was an angel. A golden angel appeared from nowhere and stole my brother's heart from his chest. You hear me? It was an angel.*"

And the crowds of onlookers erupted.

"*An angel?*" they seemed to echo as though one.

"I guess that cat is out of the bag then, sir?" Crayford said.

Noridel's reply would have made a nun blush.

7.
BEFORE THE COMMISSIONER

"**C**onfound it all to buggering hell, Noricel. Can you tell me what the bloody hell I am supposed to think when this is what stares up at me over my tea and kippers first thing in the bloody morning?"

The front page of the London Times slapped down onto the commissioner's table as if it were an accusation unto itself.

ANGELS IN SHADWELL? The headline shouted out.

BARNABUS SNELL LOSES HEART, FORTUNE

SWIFTLY FOLLOWS it carried on underneath.

"Well?"

"Well, I think that *The Times* is in desperate need of a new copy editor if the grammar of the headline is anything to go by," Noridel said archly and threw the paper back to the table with some distaste.

The Commissioner was not amused. Far from it.

"None of your bloody cheek, Noridel. This is *your* case, if someone is going to swing for this, I'll make bloody sure the noose has your name inscribed upon it before it has mine."

"I would expect nothing less, sir," Noridel said.

There was a knock on the door. A square head attached to a portly body poked through the doorway, the secretary keeping himself a safe distance behind the thick wood.

"The minister is here, sir," the head said with trepidation.

Commissioner Goldstroke reluctantly swallowed the ire he'd been aiming at his inspector, ran a finger under his collar, which suddenly looked far too tight, and straightened up.

"Send him straight through, Broadstairs,"

The head retreated with some relief.

"Keep your obstinacy and your insolence in check until the buffoon has finished, Noridel, or we'll both be banished to Civvy Street with our backsides in a briefcase," the Commissioner hissed at Noridel as they rose to their feet.

"I will try my utmost, sir," Noridel said.

Sir Columbus Creighton, the Minister of Justice, wafted into the room like a well-aimed fart. He was a man small in stature but with an arrogant self-belief bestowed upon him by a life of hereditary largesse, a sheltered and privileged upbringing that had prevented anyone having the opportunity to tell him what an arse he genuinely was. Creighton was probably reminded of his superiority every day of his life but never had need to prove it. He carried a weak chin and a face that was coloured only by the effort of raising too many a brandy to his lips.

The only thing in the man's *favour* was a splendid moustache that curled across his face as if it was desperate to escape. That moustache was more famous than the man who had cultivated it, and gave Creighton a measure of, if not favour, then at least popular notoriety amongst the public.

"That one with the daft bleedin' whiskers!"

"Now see here, Goldstroke, this simply won't do at all, you know," Creighton blustered as he entered. The minister looked around for a chair, found one and then seemed to be at a loss what to do as nobody had made any move to pull the chair out for him.

"I take it you are referring to the incident with the Snell brothers, sir?"

"Well of course I bloody am! Frightful business, Goldstroke. Snell Senior was a good friend of mine, you know, I used to lodge with the bugger frequently in the last European campaign. Fine gentleman, knew exactly how to deal with foreign devils, could handle their sinister manners better than any man I've ever known. Can't say I was too keen on the boys, mind. Pair of mollycoddled pansies if you ask me, but I think it would be very safe to say that they both enjoy Her Majesty's favour to a near exclusive degree. What the bloody hell are we going to tell her when she wakes up, eh? That one of them had his heart torn out on the streets of a slum? That the other is little more than a gibbering wreck halfway to a padded cell in Bedlam? And now the papers are spreading nonsense about *angels*?"

"The incident is most unfortunate, sir," the Commissioner simpered.

"Unfortunate? It's a damn sight more than bloody unfortunate, Goldstroke. It's a disaster, that's what it is. What were the brothers doing in so insalubrious a location in the first place?"

"I believe that they had been visiting the establishment of Madame Belvedere and her peculiar maidens."

Creighton blanched. He finally sat down behind the commissioner's desk, removing a red handkerchief from his breast pocket and dabbing at his moustache as if to comfort himself.

"I trust that this is knowledge you managed to keep concealed from the hounds of Fleet Street."

"Yes, minister."

"Then let us make certain that remains the case. Bad enough that one of the leading lights of the Empire has been slaughtered on our own doorstep, if the public learnt that he was whoring at the time, and whoring with hybrids no less, there will be outrage on the back benches. Her Majesty must never hear of this." He shoved the now dampened handkerchief back into his pocket. "Do we have any idea who killed the boy yet?"

"Not as yet, sir, no."

"Well why not, Goldstroke? Surely it can't be that hard to find the blackguard?"

Goldstroke looked as if he was actively praying

for the ground to open up and swallow him. "There are a few complications," he said meekly.

Noridel had stood in this room on many occasions as a victim of the Commissioner's red-faced tantrums at some perceived oversight at the way an investigation had been run, normally one that existed only in the mind of Goldstroke himself. How wonderful to see the man suddenly on the receiving end.

Not that he had much time for the chinless wonder providing the rebuke.

"Complications? What the blazes are you talking about, man?"

Noridel coughed into his hand. "Our killer has struck before, minister. There is a previous victim."

Creighton looked at him as if he were something that should be scraped from his boot. "And who the bloody hell are you?"

Goldstroke perked up, seeing the opportunity to deflect some of the minister's ire onto another target. "This is Inspector Thaddeus Noridel, sir. He is leading the investigation into the Snell murder."

Creighton looked him up and down and sneered through his moustache. "You haven't exactly done your profession proud so far, Noridel. Another victim, you say?"

"Yes, sir. A dock worker, killed in the same fashion the night before."

"*A dock worker?* What the bloody hell does anyone care about dock workers?"

"There were witnesses at the scene that also spoke of an angel, sir."

"Now look here, Noridel. I don't want to hear any more talk about bloody angels. Do you understand how dangerous a situation this could become? The press already have a hold of it; if we can't put a lid on this, it'll spread like the clap in a boarding house. God help us if the Vatican get wind of the notion, they'll have the Velvet Inquisition on the streets before you can say boo to a goose. A bloody angel, indeed."

"A bronze or a gold man, so say the witnesses."

Creighton glared at Noridel. "And I say *no*, Inspector. Find some anarchist revolutionary with a big mouth, or pluck some halfwit out of bedlam, hold them in front of the press and say 'Here is our man, here is our killer, nothing angelic about this squalid specimen, eh, back to work you all go'. It can't be that hard, can it?"

"And if the killer strikes again, sir?"

"Then keep a lid on it, Inspector. You appreciate that it is only ten days until Her Majesty's annual thaw?"

Noridel was only too aware of the fact.

Some years ago, at the dawn of the Eternal Empire, Her Majesty the Eternal Queen, Victoria Regina the First and Absolute, had decided that the line of royal ascension was weak. The Empire she created had begun to spread across the globe like nothing before it, the development of the military dirigible and Philosophus's breakthrough in the field of practical automata had given her a new army that the combined forces of the civilised world could do nothing to counter. Victoria had declared herself the Eternal Monarch, had placed herself in a device that kept her frozen in perpetuity, to outlive her descendents and prevent their 'weakness' from tainting the rule of her Eternal Empire.

She would reign forever, even though she would do so for but a day each year.

This naturally suited everyone else in positions of power, as it gave them 364 days a year to do exactly what they pleased just so long as they could adopt the necessary obsequiousness when she was thawed out. And the public would love her evermore, as long as that was what they were told to do.

And so, on the prescribed day, the Eternal Queen was released from her frozen throne. During this day she would take stock of her Empire, issue guidance and instruction for the coming year and eat an astonishingly hearty meal. The culinary staff at Buckingham Palace would have scoured the Earth to find new delicacies with which to impress the hungry monarch. Legend had it that she would refuse to eat the same thing twice, and that different corners of the globe were scoured each year to discover new and unusual delicacies. The Queen certainly appeared to be well fed in her brief public appearances, which did offset the rather indecorous effects of frostbite that intensified with each defrosting.

Rumour also suggested that the constant chill had begun to addle her senses. This was of course denied by the establishment, and the Queen's Thaw remained a public holiday, a day of celebration in which the monarch would address her people and grant them another year of her favour.

"It is imperative that Her Eternal Majesty hears nothing of this on her awakening," Creighton insisted. "There are important matters that she will need to proclaim upon. We must ensure that supernatural gossip does not distract her from important matters of the Empire."

"We have our very finest man on it, sir, you can be assured," the Commissioner said.

Creighton looked far from convinced. "I bloody well hope so, Goldstroke, or there will be merry hell to pay, you understand. I don't want to see any further headlines that tell me anything other than the name of the murderer and the very time we can expect to see him hanging from the gallows at Newgate. Clear it up, Inspector. As quickly as you can."

"I endeavour to do so always, Minister."

Creighton swept out of the room, his tin valet meeting him at the door to guide him back to a waiting ornithopter.

The two constabulary men waited until he was out of earshot. Then both relaxed, in their respective ways.

Goldstroke reached across his desk and retrieved a cigar which he lit with the eagerness of a drowning man sucking at fresh air.

"Sort it out, Noridel. I don't want that bumptious arse in my office again this side of Michaelmas."

"I'll do my best, sir."

~

"Why the heart, Crayford? This is what perplexes me."

Noridel turned his paperweight in his hands. It had been a gift from one of the Sexless Sages of Putney after their paths crossed in a case involving the theft of what the sages believed to be a vial of Odin's breath. It tingled beneath the fingers as though it had some electrical charge running through it, but it was an oddly relaxing sensation, like being massaged by the dancing feet of fairies.

The sages had said that a man pure of heart could see his future in the depths of the metal orb. Noridel only ever saw the reflection of his own tired face. But he liked to roll the orb in his palm, found that the action focused him, allowed him to think while the tingle of static soothed his hands.

The hands of a thinker, not a fighter. He left the fighting to Crayford.

At the moment the only thing she was fighting was a veritable mountain of paperwork, a tottering heap of files, case histories and incident reports excavated from the archives in order for a suspect list to be compiled.

As yet, she had made little progress of note. Anyone they could potentially finger for the crime seemed to have at least one mitigating factor that prevented their inclusion on the currently hypothetical list.

"Perhaps we're thinking about it all a bit too hard, sir," Crayford said,. "What if it's just some loony? Or a clockwork that's gone rogue?"

Noridel shook his head. "Why would a clockwork so specifically target the heart, though? And if it's a psychopathy then it's a very distinctive one. Rage I can understand, the desire to tear someone limb from limb. But to target the heart, the body's best-protected organ, there must be an overwhelming need that drives the assailant to attack it so directly."

"Such as what, though?"

"Well that's the thing, Crayford. If we could find out what it is that drives the compulsion then we can begin to picture the face of the creature that would hold it. What does the psychopath do? He acts out his psychopathy. He re-enacts a traumatic event. What event would lead to you wanting to remove the heart of a stranger? This is the key to it."

"Perhaps. And perhaps we should listen to what the witnesses have been telling us. I can accept you were reluctant to believe the whores, you being you and all, but the toffs aren't likely to lie, are they?"

"They were at Madame Belvedere's. Who knows what poison they smoked with those creatures."

"Still, two groups of witnesses, both say the murderer was a golden angel. Why aren't we focusing on that?" Crayford waved a hand at the tottering mound of papers. "There are no golden angels hidden inside this lot, I can tell you that. Why aren't we out there looking for our angel?"

"Because it's nonsense."

"Why? Perhaps it's someone wearing a mask. That might give us something to go on. Order some random searches of suspicious characters, see if any of them have a gold mask tucked up their tunic and a great big rusty crowbar covered in dry blood."

"To think I used to have a high opinion of you, Crayford."

"The minister is going to come crashing down on you, sir. We need to do more than just sit here and go through old case files."

"There might be something there that rings a bell, some prior incident that we can link with these current attacks."

"And I bet you a downer to a duce that we don't find a blessed thing."

"Tell you what then, Crayford, you go and do

some hunting, get your ever intuitive bobbies to stop everyone who looks at them funny and give them a good patting down. I'll stay here and give it a good think, try and actually *solve* a murder rather than stumble into its perpetrator by some stroke of unlikely fortune."

"Can't hurt to go at it both ways can it, sir?"

"I suppose not. Take care though, Crayford. There's something dark at the heart of this I fear."

She was gone, eager for action. He could hardly blame her. He'd learnt long ago that action was often just reactive, it solved nothing. It was thought that took you to the solution, the ability to map out a crime in your mind until you could see its variables, define the true path of its intent.

There was something about this case that continued to nag away at him. Something he'd seen, something that Dr Pink had said, perhaps. Since he had seen the first victim lying on the slab down in that dirty morgue, there had been a nagging thought that wouldn't come quite into focus.

Was he missing something, something blindingly obvious?

Noridel gave up. There was only one thing for it.

He would have to talk to Florence.

He plucked up the speaking tube from the wall of his office, blew into it sharply and then turned the dial.

"Switchboard," a clipped and plummy female voice said.

"Inspector Noridel here. Can you tell me where Scotland Yard is today?"

There was a brief pause as papers were consulted. "Dover," switchboard finally announced.

"It is expected to stay there for several days."\

"Excellent. Can you arrange an ornithopter to take me there as soon as humanly possible? And dial ahead and tell them that I would like to have congress with Florence."

Switchboard gave a heavy sigh as if her day had been fatally compromised. "Very well. Please make your way to the roof, Inspector, I will inform one of the fleet that you will require their services."

"Most kind," Noridel said in his most gracious manner.

"Yes," she sniffed and broke the line.

Noridel put the tube back on its hook and put on his travel coat.

"To *Dover*."

8.

IN FLORENCE'S GARDEN

There was a cold wind up on the roof even though summer had barely passed. Noridel was glad that the ornithopter was already waiting for him. The blades turned swiftly, which only added to the breeze in his face.

"Morning, sir!" said the metal half-man built into the front seat of the vehicle.

"Morning. To Dover, if you please, and Scotland Yard."

"Dover it is, sir. Would you like to avoid the wastes? It will add some time to our journey if we go the long way around."

"No, that's all right. I've got my mask with me, I'm sure I can bear an hour or so of the gypsy fumes."

"As you wish, sir."

Noridel climbed into the carriage and bolted the door shut behind him, shaking it savagely to ensure it wasn't likely to fly open mid transit. One did hear the most abominable stories about such occurrences.

The propellers of the ornithopter began to rotate faster, their thumping beat becoming a steady hum that deafened the traveller to any other sound. With a clumsy grace, the craft began to rise from the rooftop and make its way over the city toward the South Coast of England.

Noridel covered his mouth as soon as the journey began. It paid to be safe this high above the vast docks and construction sites. They pumped the residue of their industrial labour into the sky through day and night. The air up here was little more than a constant cloud of sulphur and ash and it could poison you slowly but surely.

There were no birds up here anymore; they'd long since departed for skies less tainted by the toil of humanity.

Such was progress.

Still, the city remained quite a sight, what you could see of it through the smog. They crossed the river to the south, and saw the great sprawl of the construction sites laid out beneath them like a scar upon the earth, town and country ripped asunder to provide a greater scope for the work being undertaken. Huge machines being built one metal plate at a time, their inner workings laid bare like the innards of giant beasts that had come ashore and floundered.

Vast construction giants marched across the yards, steel behemoths being puppeteered by tiny men who sat in their chests and governed their every movement. Reaching almost as high as the ornithopter flew were complex wind turbines upon which banks of canvas sails turned and converted the very air itself into the energy that would subsequently pollute it.

This was the true heart of the Empire, its factory floor. What was built here would go forth and conquer the rest of the world.

Noridel found it, as ever, awe inspiring but rather sad. His father had once had a surgery down there, in a small south London hamlet that was now just churned and violated earth. The once teeming suburbs were gone; the city of London was now circled by little more than its own scar tissue.

They flew on, past the construction sites and over the dead coal mines and the blackened site of the Last Stand of the Romany, where the forces of the Empire had scorched their own heartland to rid it of the fighting tribes of the gypsy kings. It was said that you could still smell the odour of burnt flesh in the air for miles. Noridel had tightened his face mask in preparation. He had no desire to breathe in the ashes of dead gypsies.

Still the ornithopter carried him onward, past the Canterbury Barracks, the largest site of domestic infantry in the country, an entire ancient city now converted into a military outpost. And beyond this, to the south, Noridel could see the black and churning mass that had once been the Sussex coast. It had been over a decade since the Cult of Nautilus launched the Black Coral Bomb that still to this day ate away at the land with ravenous hunger. As a boy, Noridel used to holiday at Brighton with his family. But there was no longer a Brighton beach on which to bathe, just the hungry black calcareous cancer held in check by vast viral nets to stop it from spreading across the entire island. It made one shiver to look upon its bubbling surface knowing how many poor souls it had already consumed.

Finally, Noridel saw Scotland Yard appear on the distant horizon. The yard was upright, so it towered over the landscape as a warning to wrongdoers, a giant man constructed of metal, his arms at his sides like a challenge to the world to take on his might. Where Scotland Yard walked, so justice followed. So they said anyway. Noridel had long ago learnt to ignore the hyperbole of headquarters.

It took them ten long minutes to reach the iron giant. There were a variety of docking bays built into its chest alongside the cannons and glittering searchlights that allowed it to hunt its prey wherever it might tread. The ornithopter flew inside with great care, leaving open sky behind for the oppressive ceiling of copper inside the Yard. Their entry was through a narrow tunnel that intensified the thump of the propellers into an almost unbearable volume as it bounced back at the carriage from sheer walls. Then the tunnel opened into a larger hanger, a variety of other ornithopters resting in their nests, a couple of larger zeppelins idling in their mooring stations, waiting to be deployed on their next mission. Noridel's craft came to a vacant nest, reversed slowly in and then the great blades that had carried them across the south finally ceased their rotation.

"'Ere you are, sir, Scotland Yard," the pilot said rather unnecessarily.

"Yes, thank you," Noridel said, climbing from the tight carriage and onto the gantry beyond. The air smelt of oil and helium that had leaked from the huge zeppelin balloons. A number of clockwork technicians were darting around the hanger bay on numerous tasks. They would have to be clockwork, that smell would drive a man mad within the hour.

A familiar face was waiting for him at the end of the gantry. Sergeant Asquith, a mature and rather sensible man with whom Noridel had the pleasure of working with on a number of previous cases. What Asquith lacked in humour he made up for in dedication, and Noridel found that an acceptable compromise. He would just never choose to get ran-tan in the fellow's company.

"Inspector, how goes the day?"

"Too quickly by far, Sergeant. I've been tasked to find a killer and as yet I have no idea as to what face the villain shows to the watching world."

"The Snell boy, I assume?"

"You assume right."

"You're welcome to that particular kettle of fish, Noridel. A case like that, all it's going to do is bring hell and high water down on an investigating officer. You've got my sympathies."

"Unless your sympathies were responsible for ripping the living hearts out of two innocent victims, you can bloody well keep them."

Asquith showed no signs of amusement, as was his way. He led Noridel from the hangar and made his way through a long corridor to the Nerve

Centre.

"What are you up to down here on the coast? Pirates at large still?" Noridel asked.

"No, think we've probably got most of the Gingham Pirates under lock and key now. The ringleader, Mother Tibble, has evaded our custody but it's only a matter of time. No, we've been hunting down some of the Scarlet Badger's brigade; reckon they might have set up a safe trap somewhere in the vicinity, trying to get some of the prisoners they "liberated" from Newgate out of the country and over the sea to the white mountains. No trace yet, but the chief reckons he can smell them on the wind."

"And you?"

"I dunno. They're a cunning lot, more cunning than the chief gives 'em credit for, I'd wager. They're good at setting up false trails and we're getting worse at following them. There are only a few spots they could leave the country from though, and there are steel octopi patrolling the channel. We'll have them sooner or later."

Noridel nodded his head. The work at the Yard always seemed a far cry from the petty affairs of the London streets.

"I wish you all the luck in the Empire, Sergeant. Does Ignatius know I'm coming?"

Asquith gave the closest thing to a smile his craggy face was capable of. "Oh, he knows all right. Been charging around since he heard like a bulldog with its 'ead in a wasp's nest, effing and blinding loud enough to deafen a 'orse."

"Excellent," Noridel said with something approaching delight.

The Nerve Centre was at the heart of the Yard, operation staff sitting inside a recessed pit working at desks lined with the very latest in the new-fangled computing technology that Noridel frankly had very little clue about. As far as he could make out, all these chaps and ladies were sitting behind complicated looking typewriters banging in meaningless lines of gibberish that were somehow translated by Florence into something meaningful. It was all Greek to Noridel, and no number of lectures about coding or symbols or logic patterns was going to change that.

Florence was below them somewhere, in the belly of the beast, so to speak. They had built Scotland Yard around her so as best to protect her. Not that Noridel ever felt she had the need for protection.

Asquith had let Noridel through the security doors and they had said their fond(ish) farewells. Noridel wandered across the Nerve Centre with a gait that suggested he owned the place. This, he had calculated, would drive the unwelcoming genuine project leader halfway to the madhouse.

Dr Ignatius had seen Noridel enter and had carefully ignored him for as long as he could manage without it appearing obvious. Eventually he slimed his way over to the Inspector with a smile that fooled neither of them.

"Inspector, how very nice to see you here again," he said through gritted teeth.

"I'm sure it is, Doctor. I've come to see Florence, but I'm sure you know that by now."

"I do, I do. She is most excited at the prospect. Oh, Inspector, if only we could understand what it is about you that gets her, what is it you people say so much, hot under the collar?" Ignatius's carefully practised English had begun to slip, betraying the alien origins he tried hard to conceal.

"I wish I knew myself, Doctor. I think perhaps our Florence is like any maiden of a certain age. There are certain indelicate tendencies she likes to keep secret from the prying attention of a parent."

"Florence is no child, Inspector."

"Quite. And you are no parent. But I digress, I haven't really got the time for pleasantries today. A matter of the greatest importance has brought me here and I require congress as soon as possible."

Ignatius bristled. "You do appreciate, *Inspector*, that the importance of our work here does not allow for frequent interruptions from minor officers of the law?"

"Really? Shall we ask Florence what she thinks about the matter? I'll find somewhere to sit and wait while you discuss it. I say, didn't she go on strike the last time you refused to let me talk with her?"

Ignatius surely remembered only too well what had happened the last time. It had cost his team days of work and a cartload of valuable data had been lost as a result. Florence was his creation but he was not her master, and she had made that perfectly clear.

"Very well," the doctor hissed, and led Noridel to a chamber adjoining the Nerve Centre. It was a small, undecorated room that contained nothing but a simple metal bench topped by a complicated and messy collection of colourful wire that was fixed to what appeared to a copper bowl. Without ceremony Noridel took off his coat and hopped onto the bench. He lay down, folded his hands across his chest, and closed his eyes.

"Ready when you are," he said.

Ignatius muttered foreign oaths of ill tiding quietly at the horizontal Inspector as he fiddled with the wiring. He grabbed the 'bowl' between his thin and articulate hands and pulled it down to Noridel's head, allowing the copper to slide over his crown.

"There may be some discomfort," he said, adding a whispered "*I hope*" to the end of the sentence.

Noridel didn't flinch at the prognoses. He kept his hands firmly clasped and his eyes shut.

Ignatius retreated to a protruding panel in the wall from which a lever projected. Noridel heard him pull the lever down with some force. There was an arc of current from the web of wiring, a pulse of energy that made the room throb and left the taste of electrons in motion to sour the air.

Noridel arched his back, every muscle in his body suddenly taut. Then he slumped back onto the bench like a sack of new potatoes.

"Congress achieved," he heard Ignatius say. But the doctor suddenly sounded as if he was a very long way away.

~

Noridel opened his eyes to see blue sky above him. The sound of birdsong filled his ears. He was in a garden, a lush but well-cultivated garden, on the edge of a pond whose surface rippled gently as unseen occupants popped up to get a good look at the newcomer.

He sat up; found himself slightly dampened by a

dew that didn't really exist. The sun was on his face, he could feel its gentle heat kissing him. He wasn't warm though. The artifice of Florence's garden never quite convinced him, never quite won his imagination over. The hard lessons his father had taught him on the nature of pragmatism were still etched too deeply upon his character.

"Florence?" he called across the make-believe garden. He thought he saw a hint of white billowing between the trees on the far side of the pond so he made his way toward them.

There were statues here, ancient ornaments painted in verdigris. They glared at Noridel as he passed with living eyes, but he chose to ignore their hatred. He followed the path of the flowers that Florence had planted as a trail, a maze of roses in every colour of the rainbow that proved beyond doubt that nature had played no part in the creation of this landscape. Florence's garden was not curtailed by the limits of the natural world; she could grow whatsoever she liked and see it blossom and bloom in a heartbeat.

The high hedges to either side of Noridel grew higher and now this really was a maze. The roses showed him the way through, pointing his progress to Florence and he found himself moving around corners to his left and then his right, closer together than they surely should have been, and he knew that he could never find his way out of this imbroglio of foliage unless Florence allowed it.

She was at the centre of the maze, in a courtyard carpeted with daisies, sitting upon a marble bench that could easily have been her throne. She beautiful, no that would be a ridiculous understatement. She was the epitome of beauty, she was the pinnacle of the flesh, was flawless to such a degree that not a man alive could do anything other than surrender to her favour to the abandonment of all else. She was so perfect all she could possibly be was a lie, and this was the certainty that Noridel held to when he was in her presence, that she and her garden were nothing but an illusion dancing across his synapses, a dream that Florence created and shone in his face.

Florence was a machine, a thing made of circuitry and wire, of levers and soldered iron. The garden was just an accumulation of her thoughts, a way of making tangible the impossibility of her creation.

Noridel knew this. But the sight of her never stopped hurting regardless.

"Thaddeus," she said in a voice marinated in honey. "How wonderful to see you again so soon. I count the minutes that you are gone, you know. Would you like to know how many it has been since you were last in the garden, my love? Eighty-nine thousand, two hundred and eighty. That's a very big number, wouldn't you say. I nearly lost count so many times. Why do you keep me waiting so?"

"I've been extremely busy," he said, quite pathetically.

Florence blew a raspberry through her rose red lips. "Not good enough. And you've only come to see me now because of some dreary murder you insist upon investigating. Am I not alluring enough for you, darling Thaddeus. Is there a form I should take that might better appeal to you? This, for instance."

She twirled, her white dress spinning like a carousel, and when she turned she was now a boy, as handsome as she had been beautiful, an Adonis with golden skin and hair that looked like it had been woven from gold. "Better?" she asked.

"Hardly!" said Noridel, appalled at the presumption.

"No? Oh dear. Aha, I know the very thing, what your poor neglected heart secretly yearns for."

She spun again, and when she stopped spinning she was the image of Sergeant Crayford.

"Ta-dah! Now I bet you're all aflutter my darling."

Noridel spluttered. "I have never... I would never..."

"No, darling of course you wouldn't." Florence's voice dripped with the scorn of one who can see the true colour of a man's soul. But she shook her head, and Crayford's short blonde hair was replaced with the long dark locks of Florence's chosen form.

She crossed her arms over her chest and pouted. "Go on then, ask me about your boring murder."

Noridel perked up with relief now that the familiar charades were over. She had done similar on each of his last two visits, had taunted him with images of his father and dead brother while all the time trying to soothe him with promises of her devotion. He had no idea where this devotion had sprung from or what it was based upon. He certainly hadn't done anything that he considered worthy of her overwhelming affection.

Doctor Ignatius believed it to be some sort of glitch in the intelligence centres of Florence's artificial brain. She certainly hadn't been designed to behave in this manner. Ignatius's intent had been for Florence to be nothing more than an all encompassing intelligence gathering system, into which agents of the yard could programme all data relating to criminality, the activities of suspicious parties both at home and in the newly conquered lands and any acts of sedition and terrorism. Along with this information, all and any events of cultural and social or political note were fed.

The notion was that with all this data running around in her systems, Florence would be able to detect patterns and chains of coincidence that would allow her to actively predict the possibility of crimes that had yet to take place. She would in effect give the yard the power of preemptive policing.

Florence had other ideas.

While she didn't deny to her creator or any of the other myriad experts who regularly probed her that she could indeed do exactly what it was they had designed and built her to do, and a lot more besides, she had decided that to give them that information would be cheating and they should work it out by themselves.

Rather than render herself totally useless, she gave them snippets, occasional hints of the information they required. Normally in the form of a riddle.

Concerning this murder in Wapping,
The details of which are quite shocking,
The man you require
Earns his pay by the hour
Perhaps you should check when he clocked in?

What scared Ignatius, and any other suitably

qualified boffins who had poked at her circuitry, was that she seemed to have acquired a degree of sentience far above anything they could have possibly conceived. They had begun to wonder where exactly it had come from, and just what, if any, its limitations were.

One day, Florence had printed out a schematic for a device to be constructed as an addition to her core unit. She said this was to allow 'congress'.

Ignatius's team had subsequently built this device, and found that it did exactly what she had told them it would. It allowed them to converse directly with the sentient mind of the machine they had made.

But not everyone, only a special few were allowed to walk within her garden. And one of those Florence chose to step inside her mind was named Thaddeus Noridel, even though nobody working on the Florence project had the slightest idea who that might be.

Noridel himself had no idea why the most powerful intellect in creation might have a crush on him either. But he had decided he was going to use her favour to his advantage whenever he possibly could.

"Barnabus Snell, richest man in the Empire, dead on the cobbled streets of Shadwell with his heart ripped from his chest. Ezekiel Mott, an absolute nobody half drunk on cheap gin and looking for a quick thrill down at the docks, just as literally heartless. Witnesses swear on both occasions that they have seen a man of brass, an *angel*, at the scene."

"How incredibly dreary."

"Help me, Florence. The commissioner has the minister halfway up his backside, which means he's three quarters of the way up mine."

"Ohhh, what a thought! Careful now or I'll blow a circuit. Literally."

"Come on, Florence, you don't want me booted out of the constabulary do you? It'll be a lot more than eighty thousand and however many bloody minutes until I come visit again if that happens."

"They're not going to kick you off the force, darling. Not yet, anyway," she said in a deliciously tantalising tone.

"Please, Florence. I've missed something, something that's been nagging at me since the start of this case, something I can't see."

"Rubbish. Your problem is you have seen it, *all* of it. The whole sordid thing, all in a nutshell, but your silly little brain just insists on making it all more complicated than it is."

"What do you mean?"

Florence stretched out on the marble like a lustful goddess. She yawned. "Bored now, darling. Nothing more to tell you today."

"*Florence.*"

"Tell you what, I'll tell you a little bit about what's going to happen later. I've been seeing some very odd patterns in the data. I've always known that you're special, knew it before I even saw your face. But I had no idea just how special you're going to be, how much of the future is wrapped around you."

"I don't understand, as usual. Can't you ever tell me anything that isn't wrapped in a dozen layers of enigma?"

"No! That would be no fun! And if I told you the future, think how dull it would be when it finally showed up. It'd be like hearing the punch line to an old joke, darling. No, relish the surprise!"

"I don't like surprises. They have a tendency to bite."

"Oh, then you're not going to have a lot of fun in the near future."

"Why?"

She closed her eyes, rubbed at her temples, pulling a twisted face. She spoke with a guttural, Romany accent. "I see the future... I see three boys. Perhaps they might be men but each of them will always be a boy in the eyes of others. I see what they are now, all three are *brothers*. Brothers not to each other but to others who mourn them, brothers who were lost, or perhaps they *will* be lost in the coming days. One brother went to war in a darkness of green and when he came home he was empty. Another went back to pick up the precious thing that *she* had dropped and she never saw him again. And the final brother, the most important one; he has the past in his hands and the future in his eyes. He holds the biggest secret of all, the one that changes everything. And you will have the key to unlocking it, my darling inspector. You will be the agent of the fall. Eternity will weep over your actions."

Then Florence opened her eyes and held out a hand to Noridel. "That'll be sixpence, guv'nor."

"For heaven's sake, Florence! What manner of nonsense is this?"

"The future! We'll talk about it again, don't you worry your pretty little head. And in the meantime, just because it's you; if you want to catch your killer, think about what your father tried to teach you and failed. You already saw it once; it won't take much effort to see it again. *Picture* it."

"That hardly helps me now, does it?"

"Course it does, darling. Now be off with you." She blew him a kiss that sent him spinning back through the maze like a fallen leaf in a gale. Nature curled back onto itself and the green of garden vanished as if it had been sucked down a plughole.

The garden was gone, just like that. Noridel was back on the bench with a copper bowl on his head, the smell of exotic tobacco all around him.

"Back so soon?" Ignatius said as he lounged against the wall. "Perhaps you are falling out of favour at last, yes?"

He stamped out a noxious cigarette on the floor and helped Noridel to his feet.

9.

CRAYFORD LOSES HER COOL

Sergeant Crayford had left Noridel that morning resenting the knowledge that he was inevitably right, that there was little point running off half cocked in a futile attempt to somehow force the case to a conclusion.

But she couldn't help it. She hated waiting, hated inactivity, needed to feel that she was doing something positive.

She loved being a Sergeant, loved the increased responsibility that her promotion had brought her, the chance to work on real murder cases and deal with genuine mysteries that needed solving. There wasn't a day that passed where she wasn't grateful that she had the opportunity to work with Inspector Noridel, as infuriating and obscure as he often was.

But there was a part of her that missed walking the beat, missed the feeling that every day she set foot on these cobbled, fog-obscured streets she was active, useful, a force for good in a violent and unpredictable world. Out there she could be proactive; she could prevent crime rather than detect its perpetrators. She made a difference; she was a protector rather than a mere avenger.

But today she was simply being useless.

She had asked another Sergeant, Atwell, the man responsible for the deployment of the bobbies on the beat, if any of them could be spared for a stop–and-search mission in the Shadwell district. Just two, for a few hours at the most.

Atwell shared her rank but he appeared to be at least three steps below her on the evolutionary ladder. He looked as if he had been moulded from corpulent jelly, his face a map of broken capillaries and skin mottled by the effects of many years abuse of the bottle. You could hear the booze swilling in the man's belly when he moved. He was a Desk Sergeant, and at times it was difficult to tell where the desk ended and the Sergeant began.

Atwell just laughed. "You must be pulling my chain, girl, if you think I've just got blue bottles to spare."

"I'm only asking for two. And if you call me *girl* again, Atwell, I'll pull more than your sodding chain."

Atwell looked her up and down with a leer. "Chance would be a fine thing," he said, licking his randy chops. "Times is tough on the streets, the boys is stretched as it is. I don't have any capacity to be running wild goose chases as well as chasing down the scum. Can't you get your nancy boy inspector to help you out? I hear he's never more happy then when he's patting down a dollymop. Or do you keep him entertained all by yourself nowadays?"

There was a peal of ribald laughter from the bobbies who were mooching around the office sipping tea and wasting time.

Crayford didn't want to reward the fat cretin with a reaction but there was only so much biting her tongue could take.

"Why don't you stick it right up your fat arse you drunken sot."

Atwell froze for a moment as if he didn't know what to say. And then he laughed, gobbing spit all over his incident book as he did so. "Oh you are a card! One of these days I'm gonna put you over me knee and give you such a tanning, girl, and I'll never be certain which of us would enjoy it the most!"

This raised more sniggering laughter from the bobbies.

Crayford felt her face flush with useless anger.

Atwell was one of the worst that she was forced to cope with. Dealing with him was always the same, like stepping across a cesspit, having to dodge the innuendo and the leers. Knowing that a whole conversation might go past without the other party raising his eyes from her chest, knowing that no matter how serious the matter there were always men like this who would never take her seriously as a colleague.

It still angered Crayford when this happened, but not as much as it once had. She had become used to it, and as Noridel told her time and again, she had already proved she was worth ten of the likes of Atwell; she didn't have to go on proving herself. There was nobody left to convince.

But Noridel didn't really know her half as well as he thought he did.

She dug deep into the back of her throat, managed to hack up something thick and heavy. Without pause she tugged the incident book across the desk and spat the whole mouthful of phlegm into the centre of the half completed page. Then she slammed the cover shut.

Atwell turned a whole new shade of purple.

"You filthy scratch-an-itch! I'll have you on a charge, just you see if I don't!" he called at her, peeling his book open to reveal the sticky mayhem inside as she stormed out of the station.

This time Crayford didn't respond.

~

Crayford decided not to return to Noridel's office straight away.

She was hot under the collar. The stupid anger that never got her anywhere, it just made her more enemies when she already had enough to burn. Now she'd given Atwell a reason to complain, and the story would be all round the station with his spin on it by the time she got back. Noridel would have her back, the complaint wouldn't go anywhere, of that she had no doubt. But he'd got the upper hand now, he'd riled her and now he and every other cretin in the force would be lining up to do it again, to see what she'd do next time.

She'd let herself down. She could have punched the wall in frustration, but it would be a poor substitute for Atwell's beefy face. Better if she did her job, got out there and found some answers. Prove herself again, even if it was only for her own benefit.

The previous day she had wasted precious hours asking questions that were never likely to be answered fully of both the docking guilds and that had gotten her nowhere. The guilds had little interest in crimes that did not pay them a dividend.

But Crayford had one more source of information to turn to.

A few streets away from the station, underneath a gaslight that always flickered but never went out, there was a Constant Vendor.

Nobody saw as much, nobody heard as much and nobody missed as little as they did. And this particular one seemed to have a soft spot for Crayford. The vendor had become her own secret informant, and having him whispering knowledge of the streets into her ear had been an important factor in her zipping her way up the greasy pole of promotion.

"*GET YOUR TIMES! YOUR STANDARD! YOUR NEW FINANCE*," the vendor blared out. These were the names of the newspapers he sold from the kiosk his legless trunk was bolted to. The papers were printed on brittle yellow paper; paper that had been pulped and recycled so many times it would have consumed the ink pressed into it by the time you'd gotten to the obituaries. And everyone knew they were always the best bit of the whole ruddy paper.

"Evening, Burt," Crayford said to the vendor.

Its head spun round to her. It had been given a rudimentary face, a metal grille for a mouth, a pointed nose that was in fact a clasp to keep the head unit in place, two yellow eyes with once black pupils, the paint now melted away to little more than a shadow by the bulbs that lit them. He wore a cap on his head, a gift from Crayford that he had never taken off since. That hat was his proudest possession.

"Hello—*STANDARD*—Sergeant," he stuttered, the voice box in his chest glitching into auto-vendor mode as usual. "Wanna paper? On the house of course, I won't take a penny from me most favourite copper."

"What would I read in a paper that I don't already know?"

"Now that's a good question. You can't even wipe your arse with it, anymore, paper's getting—*STANDARD. GET YOUR EVENING STANDARD*—getting so rough."

"I'm a Sergeant now, Burt. I get someone else to wipe my backside for me."

Burt wheezed and wobbled back and forward in his kiosk, an automaton's equivalent of laughter. "I can't think of no finer job for a young constable," he crackled.

"I need to consult your nose, Burt."

"Well there ain't none—*LONDON TIMES*—none finer, sergeant."

"Have you smelt anything on the wind about the murders?"

"The angel murders? The thing what done for that rich nob?"

Crayford winced. "That's the business. Although the inspector has a bit of a paddy if anyone mentions an angel."

"S'alright. I just heard some of your—*GET YOUR—GET YOUR—GET YOUR*—bobbies chatting about it. The gutter press don't have a whiff of it yet. They don't even know them two killings is linked. Too worried about whipping up folk into a frenzy about—*STANDARD*—the bloody Queen, if you'll mind me French."

"So, anything?"

"I ain't so sure. It's a bit of a weird one. But you know what your Inspector says, the rude fellow. Ain't nothing is a coincidence."

"He does say that on occasion." He also said that only fools can see patterns in the sand, but Crayford had become accustomed to his contradictions.

"Well then. You know the dossers who sleep over the way on the site of the old fishery, you wouldn't want to get too—*GET YOUR STANDARD*—close to them, I can even smell them and my olfactory unit is deader than Dead Prince Eddie. Anyways, something's upset them. They was all set up over there, ain't nobody interested in the site, been left all alone for months it has, got themselves a proper little village of rag and bone."

Crayford did know. They were due to be cleared out the following week; she'd heard a few constables begging for a place on the crew. The rules on necessary aggression went out the window when the subject was a mumper. Fair game for the baton.

"Well they all up and left it, couple of days ago,

went off like someone had put a—*LONDON TIMES. GET YOUR LONDON TIMES*—put a burning Whirlitzer up their behinds. They was proper spooked, Sergeant."

"Any idea why?"

"Don't exactly have many cosy chats with them that don't involving them begging me for a coin or two. But I would have thought it must be some right devilry to force them out of their cosy little nest."

"That's useful, Burt. Probably nothing to do with the case, but it's useful all the same."

"You know me, Sergeant; I like to keep an ear to the—*STANDARD*—ear to the—*STANDARD*—ear to the—*GET YOUR LONDON TIMES*—ear to the ..."

"Ground, Burt?"

"You really do know me, Sergeant."

~

Noridel had spent the journey back from Dover in something of a stupor. Florence tended to have that effect on a man. He'd told the ornithopter driver to take the long way round, deciding that he had enough dead gypsy in his nostril for one day. But he couldn't concentrate, couldn't find the peace he needed to focus. Florence had unnerved him, given him too much to think about coupled with a plug tail stiff as a yard arm that even the most well tailored of trousers was unlikely to conceal. Another good reason for the detour. To allow his passions to cool.

The most infuriating thing about Florence was that she was always right. She might obscure the truth in all sorts of unnecessary fancy, but the truth was what remained when you unpeeled it all.

From the very start of this case there had been an itch at the back of Noridel's mind, one that he had been simply unable to scratch, something crawling about in his unconscious but unwilling to make the leap to the surface. The hunt for the truth was causing him pain in his shoulders, a slow tension that he would soon have to relieve.

Not so long ago, he would have retreated to a pleasure house and gotten a metal Piston Lass to work out the tension for him. This tended to work a treat, but just the previous month he had worked a case with the aid of Jerry Mander, the canine-hybrid detective who the constabulary often turned to in cases involving non-human suspects and who had become something of a good friend to Noridel, despite his tendency to suddenly hump the inspector's leg without the slightest provocation.

It had turned out that a number of corpses they'd found stuffed into furnace shoots near the pleasure district had been placed there by unscrupulous owners of malfunctioning automata which had rather over-stimulated the clients they had been relieving of a variety of 'tensions'. Noridel was now rather more cautious about putting any of his vulnerable flesh in the hands of anything that ticked, tocked or whirred.

He rubbed the back of his neck with his own hands, failing to do much good and pinching his skin in the process. Perhaps he could train Crayford to apply the required pressure to the necessary spots. The notion amused him. He'd probably be safer with the Piston Lass.

He returned to his office and rubbed at his paperweight in an effort to stimulate the grey cells.

The diagram that Dr Pink had provided of the first victim's wounds lay on the desk, the scarlet stains of real blood that had dropped from the doctor's never-clean hands all too prominent upon the paper. Arrows pointed to marks on the body, comments inserted where the doctor had found points of interest.

But it was the diagram itself that was calling to Noridel, not the detail.

Since he returned from his outing to consult Florence he had devoted all his mental energy to pondering the case and the diagram had absorbed much of that attention. He sensed he was close to the knowledge he sought, but still he couldn't quite see it. It was there in the shape of that template the doctor had provided, the frame of the human form, the limbs and major organs marked clearly for aid of the ignorant. Some detail he'd missed. If he could just see what it was!

If only he could picture it. That was what Florence had said.

Picture it.

And suddenly he did.

It wasn't the detail, of course! That wasn't the point at all. He'd been looking at it all wrong. It was the diagram itself, not the injuries that Dr Pink had carved onto it with his quill. The diagram. The human form, the location and arrangement of organs.

The arrangement of the organs!

"By Lucifer. Of course," he cried, shot to his feet, donned his overcoat and sped from the station.

10.
THE FIEND REVEALED

The old fishery was gloomy.

The windows had been torn out so that the metal frames could be sold for smelt. The long chamber which ran along its length, that had once been home to a line of single-function automata slicing, dicing and filleting the produce of the sea, was now bare but for the debris of machinery torn from its moorings and the overwhelming stench of the millions of fish that had passed through on their way to the markets of Covent Hyper-Garden and beyond.

That odour wormed its way relentlessly into

Crayford's nostrils, but it did at least obscure the fainter but more pungent stenches that the occupancy of the squalid beggars had left behind.

Crayford held up her lamp and let the yellow arc of light spread across the chamber. There was nothing here, the chamber was dirty and abandoned and if anything had scared the tramps away it had followed after them.

A rat scurried across the floor, stopped halfway across and turned to look at Crayford, bold and imperious, confident that this empty shell was its domain and not hers.

Crayford threw a handful of rubble at the rodent and watched it scuttle away into the gloom. She noticed that there was a red light flashing on the wall at the far end of the chamber, faint but regular. She moved toward it, the lamp lighting her way. It was an automatic winding station, a simple recess in the wall into which one of the clockwork automata stationed here could place its winding lever and have it turned, recharging it without the need for a human winder on site.

These stations had caused a lot of unrest with the Guild of the Flesh, she remembered. Her father was a man of the Guild. *Was* a man of the Guild. She wondered what he would have made of such a thing, another device designed to take away a function from the working man and give to a machine. He would have had a fit, then gotten drunk, then hurt someone, most probably Crayford.

If she was lucky.

She lifted the lamp higher and saw the huddled shape on the floor behind the winding station. The shape of a man, sprawled across the floor, dead eyes staring at the ceiling, filthy clothes torn away from his upper body, a ruination of flesh and bone exposed to the elements. Heart clumsily removed. The rat sat in the cavity of his chest, its sharp teeth gnawing at bone, gore glistening on its chin. It looked at Crayford, bold as before.

Look, it seemed to be saying, *this is what I wanted you to see, it's mine but you can share if you* really *want to.*

Crayford kicked out at the creature and it bolted away. A number of thoughts occurred to her as she looked at the ravaged tramp and the flashing light of the winder, and those thoughts swiftly gathered themselves together and created a picture, a picture she suddenly found very disturbing.

She had to get out of there and find the Inspector. She turned back to the entrance.

The figure that had crept up behind her shot out a powerful hand and giant fingers wrapped around her neck before she could resist.

Crayford was lifted from the ground, her feet kicking at air. She couldn't breathe, her fingers clawed at the hand that choked her, and found it was metal, pitted and scarred but tough and immovable.

She looked into the face of the creature that strangled her, and saw her own reflected back at her, distorted in the dull bronze. The head was shaped like a man's, but there were deep groves and indentations, as if the surface had been repeatedly hammered out of shape over time. On what should have been the face there were the traces of painted features, the detail now almost gone. Wrapped over its shoulders was an old blanket, smeared in oil and dirt of a dozen descriptions. The blanket flapped from its broad body like wings.

The sort of wings you might see on an angel.

And with that thought, Crayford realised how much trouble she was in.

She could feel consciousness fading, and the cold touch of the monster's other hand on her chest told her that she would never wake up again, that her heart was to be surrendered up to her aggressor, that her sleep would begin on Dr Pink's autopsy table, the latest victim of a homicidal automaton. Just what she had said it was from the start. She wanted to scream her rage at it, to go not quietly into death but fighting every inch of the way down.

But she had no breath left to do so.

Had Noridel arrived as little as ten seconds later, she might never have breathed again.

He leapt from the shadows as spring heeled as any legendary jack, wrapping an arm around the angel's shoulders. In one swift movement he used the other hand to thrust his paperweight inside the hollow alcove that lay in the middle of its trunk, an empty hole just the right size for the sage's gift.

Noridel fell from its shoulders onto the hard floor. A fizz of static singed the air.

The angel's fingers became taut, their grip on Crayford released. She fell to the concrete floor, blue faced and bruised, wheezing as precious air was once again allowed in. Noridel was with her in an instant, helping her breathe.

"Relax, Crayford. Deep breaths, long deep breaths."

She fought the panic in her desperate throat and did as he said, air filling her lungs, the pounding in her head starting slowly to calm. She leant forward and vomited onto Noridel's shoes.

"It's a good thing I didn't wear suede today, Crayford, or you would be facing an extensive bill for cleaning and repair," he said into her ear, rubbing her back tenderly. "And you also owe your conspiratorial vendor a new hat as thanks for his concern at your wellbeing. Without that concern, I may never have found you."

Above them the bronze angel shaped like a man staggered in a pattern of ever decreasing circles before it eventually collapsed to the floor, its limbs finally at rest.

~

"It was the diagram, you see. I was looking too hard at the detail, when it was the template itself that was telling me what I already knew."

"I see," Crayford said, though she didn't see at all.

"My father, as you know, was a physician. And he taught. He taught well, was famous for it. And I can remember one time he let me join a group of his students for one of his demonstrations, he was desperate for me to follow him into medicine, hated the idea of me joining the constabulary. He would have done anything in his power to stop me if he thought it would have done a blind bit of good.

"So anyway, this session was on something to do with ailments of the kidney, or liver, or some such, I can hardly remember the details. And what he used for this demonstration, what the students used to train on, was this."

He held up the diagram of the body and its many

organs that Dr Pink used.

"A picture?"

"No. They used a basic automaton, but this is in effect what it was. It was a construct with removable organs, its chest plate could be removed as if it were a ribcage and the internal organs were laid out to replicate a human, each of them made from hollow tin and each of them exactly to scale. The idea was that you could practice any of the basics of surgery on this machine, it was designed to familiarise students with human biology. You could open the wretched thing up and take out its heart, its lungs or its liver. And then put them all back, obviously."

"So how do we get from there to murder, sir? Why was it killing people?"

"Well Crayford, that's the rub. It seems the teaching faculty at Charing Cross have developed a number of far more effective training devices in the years since my father was lording it over the staff there. Our 'murderer' was thrown on the scrap heap, ready for the smelts, useless to them. But nobody took the time to turn the ruddy thing off. They left him there, still functioning, and before he was dumped, some bright spark dug in his chest and plucked out the tin heart. Decided to keep it as a memento. Or perhaps even a paperweight." He looked down with renewed fondness at the now singed orb resting on the tabletop.

"I see! So our angel wakes up who knows where—"

"And he's missing a heart. So he decided to go and look for one."

"But the ones he finds aren't made of tin and they

don't fit quite right. No matter how hard he squeezes them in, they keep falling out."

"He would have gone on looking until his circuits failed. Heart after heart after heart."

"A properly heartless killer."

"Indeed, Crayford."

"I said it was an automaton, didn't I? Right from the start. You and your high-faluting ideas, you reckoned you knew better."

Noridel rose from his seat and bowed to his sergeant. "And I salute your superior intelligence. Never again shall I question your wisdom, Crayford."

"Chance would be a fine thing."

"In the meantime, I shall go and give my full report to our rather relieved Commissioner and take full credit for the entire undertaking. You, I believe, have a rather indecorously defaced incident report book to painstakingly reconstruct."

Crayford left to undertake her task with due ill grace. Noridel smiled at her back as she left, grateful that the events of the day had not left her with anything other than bruises and dented pride.

He felt that he would be quite lost without her.

The speaking tube whistled on the wall behind him.

"Noridel," he lifted the receiver and announced.

"Darling, I knew that you'd find the answers. Wasn't such a tough puzzle after all, was it?"

"Florence? How on earth can you contact me in such a manner? I thought this device only worked for communication within the station?"

"Oh, I keep on discovering new things I can do!" Her voice was as clear as if she was standing on the other side of the desk, even though Noridel knew that her voice was simply a ghost in a machine that walked the land a hundred miles away from where he sat. "Some of those things would turn your hair white, darling. But what does it matter. I just wanted to give you my congratulations, and remind you not to wait so long until you come and visit again. I've seen some very odd things in the patterns I've been following that make me worry about you ever so much. "

"What things?"

"Oh I can't tell you! That would be cheating. You should know that by now. But if I were you, I wouldn't put things off until after Christmas. Remember darling, three brothers and the sorrow they bring. Eternity will weep because of what you do. Ta-ta for now, don't keep me waiting long!"

And she was gone.

Noridel replaced the receiver, and his thoughts were very much of the future.

EPILOGUE

In the heart of the vast smelting plants, where anything that had once been useful was melted down and reformed so that it might be useful again, the golden/bronze automata that for a while had been thought of as an angel lay on a rubber conveyor belt heading for its doom.

Still some forty feet from the furnace, it had already begun to notice the effect of the heat. The surface coating of golden paint that had rusted gently for years had started to blacken and flake away. Its internal temperature had started to rise and the last few functional circuits began to burn away.

Next to it on the conveyor was an old copper battery, orb shaped, its purpose long forgotten. The angel reached for it, hands blistering as it retrieved the object. It raised it above its chest, and then jammed it as hard as it could into the empty hole where its heart used to be. The organs around it buckled but it stayed in place.

It fit.

If the angel had been capable of smiling, it would finally have done so.

ABOUT THE AUTHOR

Jonathan Templar lives in Cheshire, UK. He has written a growing body of dark and speculative fiction, and his work had been included in a number of highly acclaimed anthologies from a variety of publishers.

Jonathan's first collection of stories, 'The Geometry of Hell', will be published later in 2013 and he is currently beavering away on further adventures for Inspector Noridel.

You can find out more at www.jonathantemplar.com Please bring snacks.